MATTI RÖNKÄ

periscope
www.periscopebooks.co.uk

A Man with a Killer's Face

First published in Great Britain in 2017 by

Periscope
An imprint of Garnet Publishing Limited
8 Southern Court, South Street
Reading RG1 4QS

www.periscopebooks.co.uk
www.facebook.com/periscopebooks
www.twitter.com/periscopebooks
www.instagram.com/periscope_books
www.pinterest.com/periscope

1 2 3 4 5 6 7 8 9 10

Translated from the Finnish *Tappajan näköinen mies* (Gummerus 2002)
by David Hackston

This work has been published with the financial assistance
of the Finnish Literature Exchange (FILI).

FILI FINNISH LITERATURE EXCHANGE

ISBN 9781859641781

A CIP catalogue record for this book is available from the British Library.

This book has been typeset using Periscope UK,
a font created specially for this imprint.

Typeset by Samantha Barden
Jacket design by James Nunn: www.jamesnunn.co.uk

Printed and bound in Lebanon by International Press:
interpress@int-press.com

Pakila, Helsinki

The woman said her name to her reflection: 'Sirje'.

Her mouth moved in exaggerated emphasis, as though she were talking to a deaf person. She applied a swipe of lip balm, then pressed her lips together, pursing and releasing them in turn.

She was a dark-haired, almost beautiful woman. When they met her, men never knew whether to call her a girl or a woman, though she was already old enough to be the kind who enjoyed reading glossy women's interior-design magazines.

Sirje brushed her smooth, shoulder-length hair, finally seemed content after the umpteenth stroke of the brush, then hid her hair in a thin, green woollen scarf. She buttoned up her coat, rocked back and forth from her toes to the heels of her boots, flicking the buckle on her satchel open and shut in the same tempo.

Then Sirje let out a sigh, pulled on her leather gloves, working the sheaths of each finger into place until they sat snugly, and made to leave. At the door she took one last glance in the mirror, but didn't look back around the hallway or the house that had become so familiar; she didn't inhale its scent, didn't pause in concentration until her ear finally homed in on the low clack of the grandfather clock in the living room and the hum of the fridge-freezer in the kitchen.

No; she merely smiled at the mirror, mouth slightly askew, as though she were smirking at a private joke. She carefully clicked the door shut, locked it, shutting off the house's dry, centrally heated air from the sharp, damp cold outside, and walked across the garden to the street, her boots crunching in the snow.

Kesälahti, Eastern Finland

Yura's job was simple: stay awake. That was it. That's what Karpov had told him to do, and Yura had given his word. Maybe the job was just too easy. Even Yura yearned for something a bit more demanding.

A portable worksite cabin had been brought inside the industrial warehouse to form a makeshift office; that's where Yura was to sit. To sit and drink tea from a Thermos flask, eat bread, tinned meat and chocolate. And smoke. 'There's plenty of smokes in there, so long as you don't torch the building,' Karpov had smirked.

Funny boss, Karpov. Sometimes he chatted and rambled in Finnish, of which Yura couldn't understand a word. Still, even in Russian he made peculiar jokes and laughed too much. He was an odd character. And besides, a place like this, nothing but sheet metal and concrete – how could this place go up in flames?

'If something happens, Yura, then you call me. But remember: stay awake, all the time, all night, all day, all evening.'

Karpov had harped on, repeating the same thing over and over, and Yura had nearly snapped at him: 'Yes, all right! Got it.'

Needless to say, Yura had dozed off. And when he woke up, he knew at once that things had turned sour – very sour. The frozen air had pushed its way into the office, and his sleepy skin felt the chill.

The warehouse doors are open, Yura thought, though his mind was as stiff with sleep as the gearbox of a truck jumpstarted in a snowdrift, beating the engine oil into motion one cog at a time. *Is oil an amorphous material?* Surprised that he even knew such a word, Yura shook off the thought, which was to be his last.

As a child, Yura hadn't dreamed of becoming a cosmonaut or a teacher or even an engine driver or a successful criminal. Other kids had always been faster, stronger, smarter, and Yura knew this only too well. He was happy as long as he could eat a decent meal regularly, drink himself into oblivion, get laid every now and then and find a mattress and a blanket for the night in a relatively warm room. Karpov had taken good care of him these last few years, and Yura didn't have any great plans for the future.

But he had certainly imagined living longer than twenty-six years. This was not good, not at all. A man was standing a metre in front of him, a tall man in a blue Adidas tracksuit, a hat on his head, his hand raised and pointed steadily at Yura. And in his hand, fifty centimetres from Yura's forehead, was a black pistol.

Tallinn, Estonia

The room was tidy, open and brightly lit, though it had originally been built as a storage space, a garage or workshop. The walls had been plastered and smoothed, then painted white; the grey steel shelves were sturdy but unremarkable, and the tidy concrete floor sloped gently and immaculately towards the floor drains.

Working around a set of melamine tables, wearing white coats, were five men and one woman, each weighing measures of white powder into plastic bags, sealing the mouths of the bags and wrapping them in aluminium foil. They worked as though at a conveyor belt in a production line, silently and efficiently.

In the middle of the room stood a man, his posture guarded and calculated, doling out commands. 'Move the boxes of mobile phones over there. Tidy up that package, lads, and let's be bloody careful with that powder.'

The man was neither old nor tall, and his voice wasn't loud; but he was used to ordering people around, and he clearly relished it.

His employees were happy to obey him. They knew their boss was sensible and wise, cunning even. He had been loyal to his people – something pretty rare in this business. Many bosses took a cut for themselves and stabbed their business partners in the back or took unwise, insane risks – and many ended up abusing the stuff themselves.

But not this boss. He had dealt in women, copper, tin and firearms as well as passports and visas. But it was just business, services and merchandise for sale, nothing more, he was keen to remind them. His own wife, pistols and papers were for his exclusive use. He had never even tried drugs, and didn't find anything strange about this in the slightest.

Sometimes he gave a contented sigh at the thought of how nice and clear-cut it was, dealing with money and stolen goods. As for women with whips, hormones to make your muscles bulge and substances that mess with your head – he didn't like that. Money kept flowing in, much more than he would earn in small-time petty theft.

Transportation, packaging and storage, logistics right the way from Afghanistan to Russia, onwards to Tallinn and from there into Finland, the entire chain of command rolled, smooth and slick, from one cog to the next. And on the way, the opium of the poppy fields was refined into pure, high-end heroin.

The small man with the upright posture was proud of his business.

Sortavala, Russian Karelia

Anna Gornostayeva tested the soil with her finger, then watered the geranium. She nattered away to herself, though she'd often noted sardonically that around here you only needed your mouth for eating. There was nobody to hear her chitchat except the flowers and the photographs, no dogs or cats in the old house – and no mice either, thank goodness.

She straightened the curtains and ran her hand along the smooth, embroidered tablecloths, then wondered whether or not to give the rugs a shake; but she knew there was no dust in them to shake off. *Why, I've got to keep a tidy house,* Anna Gornostayeva thought. *Life needs a structure, a rhythm to hold on to.*

From the large pot on the stove, which was always warm, she ladled some hot water into a bucket, cooled it with water from the pail, dampened a threadbare cotton towel that had now been designated a rag and began wiping away the imaginary dust from the photographs in the bedroom.

'Niilo, Nikolai, my little Kolya,' she whispered, tenderly caressing her husband's photograph. She berated him gently: 'Why do you still insist on turning up in my dreams…? Stay away, will you?' Then she replaced the photograph atop the chest of drawers. The man in the image had a straight nose, and his face was soft even without airbrushing. His eyes – she remembered them above everything else. She could remember them even without the photograph: eyes like those of an innocent forest animal.

Those same heavy eyes appeared in the boys' photographs too, images taken during their time in the army. The shine of the visors on their peaked caps and the stiffness of the thick fabric of their uniforms recurred through the decades. Their chests were laden with medals and accolades – their father had the most impressive collection – and, although the photographs were black-and-white, you could sense the deep, festive red of the stars on each of those medals.

Anna Gornostayeva didn't complain. At this age, she was used to being alone; she even enjoyed it, though dizziness and a strange chest pain often took her by surprise and gave her a fright. But now she felt strangely restless, and didn't know why.

Of course, the boys usually telephoned her and worried about her: 'Don't chop firewood by yourself, and don't go climbing up that ladder either. Why can't you just heat the house with the electric radiators?' They chided her and bossed her around as they would a child. They meant well, of course, but you couldn't take them all that seriously, Anna chuckled to herself. After all, she was a grown woman, her mind intact, a woman who had lived through the war and all that had followed.

But nothing terrible could have happened to the boys, she reasoned. Alexei will surely get on well enough in Moscow; he has a good wife, his son is grown up and things at work seem fine. Viktor has been used to looking after himself from a young age. Finland is a foreign country, of course, but that's where he wanted to go. He managed to get in, and it always seems that his life there is fine and dandy.

Don't worry, Anna told herself. There's no point spending the spring worrying about the autumn rains. And if you spill the milk, you can milk the cows again tomorrow… Proverbs started popping into her mind, so much so that she lost her train of thought and told herself out loud not to be so silly.

She started to polish Viktor's prizes: small gleaming cups, spoons and round medallions attached to ribbons. Her left arm ached. *Have I been sleeping awkwardly and caught a chill?* Anna Gornostayeva wondered.

1

I noticed the man some way off. He was striding towards my office with shallow steps, like an orienteer whose next flag was on the edge of my desk. I took my feet off the desk, squinted and tried to follow the dark, featureless figure. Against the light, Hakaniemi Square looked bright. The sun shone across the square; the sight was like a faded photograph in a family album titled *The family on a square in Agadir.*

Many of my clients hesitate at the corner of the square or the narrow strip of park – nothing but sand, a few benches and a tree – and meander round to my office. They often wear a fur hat and a dark overcoat, and need help with a nationalization application or with filling in housing-benefit forms. I help them.

Then there are those who are Finnish builders, truck drivers or fitters, men whose wives, fifteen years their junior, have had enough of their red-bricked semi-detached prisons in deepest suburbia. Irina or Natasha or whatever their names were had packed up their things, taken the kids and headed back to their families in the Verkhoyansk district. It's my job to track down the runaways.

A few clients might pull up on Viherniemenkatu in their Mercedes and BMWs without the slightest care. They leave the engines running on the double-yellow lines and leave their girls in leather skirts to keep an eye on the furry dice. These are businessmen whose staff have been seized, deported or taken into rehab. They might need a courier service or someone trustworthy to go over their purchase conditions. I have an honest face.

This client was something else. I didn't have time to give the matter much thought before he was inside, without knocking, striding the few steps from the street into my office.

'Viktor Kärppä…'

The sentence was left unfinished, without a question mark, and hung in the air like a haiku.

'That's me,' I nodded and tried to look grateful and businesslike. The man's appearance was neat and clinical: pressed, dark-grey trousers, the kind of black shoes that fashion magazines called 'sensible' and a green oilskin trenchcoat that had probably never seen a sea breeze. The man clasped his cap and gloves in one hand and set his rectangular briefcase on the floor between a chair and his leg. Ex-military, I guessed, but which army? A visiting businessman? A solicitor from an entrepreneurial organization, or an inspector from the city council?

I was hoping the man might be a client. I tried to have as little to do with society as possible. The police were the only state officials I had any contact with, and a regular policeman wouldn't have come alone. The man was too old to be a field officer for the intelligence services, and besides, there was no stripped, modest trademark Volkswagen Golf parked outside.

'Aarne Larsson,' he introduced himself. 'I understand you can take care of certain, shall we say, *problems*.'

Even his voice was dry. It wheezed in his parched throat like the grate of snow beneath a set of unwaxed skis. His presumption was more or less factually correct, I suppose. I decided not to bother giving him any specifics.

'I've got a problem, a rather unfortunate situation... Well, to be blunt: my wife has disappeared.'

Larsson was eyeing up my office. From the bookshelf he picked up *The Concise History of Finland* and volumes V and VI of the red-covered *Encyclopaedia of General Knowledge*. I was annoyed that I'd just returned the first volume of Pentti Saarikoski's biography to the library; now *that* would have looked sophisticated lying open on my desk.

'You might be able to help me, using your... contacts. You see, my wife is Estonian. She moved to Finland in the early Nineties,' the man explained, his speech slow but deliberate.

'I hear you have an extensive network among people who have moved here from the former Soviet Union,' he said, his grey expression fixed on my eyes. I couldn't tell whether he meant this as an accusation or a compliment, so I said nothing.

Larsson sat down in the better of my client chairs. Spring sunshine gleamed on the linoleum floor, baking old stains that refused to be wiped away. The previous tenant of my office had been from a local trade-union division, and I'd bought the union secretary's desk and filing cabinets after realizing they had left permanent dents in the flooring. The generous trade unionists had thrown a few more bits of ancient paraphernalia into the deal for posterity. The shoes of hundreds of visitors had scuffed the linoleum in precisely the same spot and left indelible black streaks across the floor.

I looked back at Larsson, trying to appear honest and expressionless, and waited. The silence heightened the tick-tock of the Chinese alarm clock on my desk. A voice on the radio was reading the shipping forecast in humble, mellow tones. When it reached the island of Gotska Sandön, I decided to speak.

'Perhaps you could give me a few basics first, then we'll see whether or not I can help you. This is all confidential, of course. I won't use this information for anything else, even if you decide not to hire me.' It was my standard opening line, and I knew it by heart. I opened my notebook.

'I've already made notes of all relevant events and background information,' Larsson cut in. He had obviously decided to take control of the situation from the outset. He flicked open his briefcase and handed me a sheet of paper, neatly printed out and protected by a brightly coloured plastic sheath.

'This should give you all the facts,' he said, and took out his glasses.

I read the lines of justified text very carefully. Larsson was no civil servant; he owned a second-hand bookshop on Stenbäckinkatu in the Töölö neighbourhood. 'Near the old sporting association building. Well, it was probably before your time...'

'Not at all, I go swimming there sometimes,' I said.

'I specialize in historical literature, political movements, that sort of thing. I don't deal in prose at all, or any other modern fiction for that matter,' Larsson continued unwaveringly, studying my face as though trying to discern which section of his text I had reached. He didn't say this in mockery or disdain – but it was clear that he respected facts, not fiction.

From his date of birth I calculated that Larsson was in his sixties, and that Sirje, his missing wife whose name

I now read for the first time, was thirty-five years old. They had been married for six years and had no children. Larsson had been married before, but this had ended in divorce. His ex-wife and high-school-aged son lived in Lahti.

Larsson had dutifully provided his home address. I tried to place the street, and judging by the door number – without a letter to indicate a stairwell – I concluded that he lived in a detached house in the Pakila area of Helsinki. There was also mention of a summer cottage in Asikkala, and he had listed a small group of relatives and business contacts. The document was a typed-up version of the notes I had been ready to take.

Larsson bent down and took another white envelope from his briefcase. From it, he produced a photograph. For the first time he seemed slightly wary. 'This is Sirje. It was taken last summer…'

I took the photograph. The dark-haired woman was looking directly at the camera. The wind had blown her hair in front of her face, and she was about to brush the loose curls from her cheek. Her mouth was set in a half-smile. Behind her you could see rocks, the shoreline and the crashing of waves. Sirje's face was pleasant, her eyes dark; but her gaze was somewhat downcast, unassuming and modest rather than self-assured.

A memory from the past caught me off-guard, bored its way through my concentration and pricked my mind, leaving me unsteady, wired, light-headed. Pine needles on the path through the island in Lake Ladoga, the grey sand on the shore, the girls in bare feet. Everything seemed fresh and crisp, as though these emotions and sensations had been suddenly taken from a freezer and left to thaw. I tried to clip the memories before they had a chance to focus, to join together and find the coordinates in my mind, then tug at my chest with longing. I forced myself to return to the matter of Aarne Larsson and the photograph of Sirje Larsson.

'An attractive woman.'

Larsson's look of bewildered satisfaction took me by surprise. I placed the photograph on the table and reread the paperwork he had drawn up.

'When did your wife disappear and when did you realize she was missing? Were there any particular circumstances under which she disappeared? I assume you've been in contact with the police?'

'Sirje disappeared on 6 January. I was at the bookshop. She'd left home some time that afternoon without mentioning anything in particular. And she didn't take anything out of the ordinary with her. I waited that evening, asked friends if they'd seen her, called her family in Tallinn, then called the police and reported her missing. No one seems to have seen her. I've tried hotels, border controls, ferry terminals, the airport. There's nothing; not a trace.'

Larsson spoke as though he were reciting a prepared statement. He sat quietly, upright; only his voice seemed reticent.

'And the police simply called off their investigation. I tried to reason with them and lay down the law, but they all but laughed in my face. They made it abundantly clear that a missing Estonian woman was not worth their time. They didn't say as much, but that's what they meant.' Larsson's voice tightened. 'Let the criminals sort out their own mess – that's what they were thinking. But I know Sirje wouldn't ever get involved in anything illegal. And that's why I've come here. I hope you can find her.'

Larsson could see me staring at Sirje's details in the paperwork he'd provided. At first I'd just glanced over it. Now I understood why the police had reacted the way they did. As though reading my thoughts, Larsson said, 'Yes, Sirje's maiden name is Lillepuu. Her brother is Jaak Lillepuu.'

2

Gennady Ryshkov waved Sirje's photograph and shook his head. 'Jaak Lillepuu's sister? Never met her. But I don't use the Estonian girls, and I don't know them. I've never seen this one working the streets in Helsinki.'

I snatched the photograph from Gennady's fingers and put it back in the folder. Ryshkov lit a cigarette and flicked the ash neatly into a round, copper-coloured ashtray with the words LAHTI SPECIAL embossed on the bottom. This, too, I had inherited from the trade unionists when I'd moved into the office. The chain round Ryshkov's wrist jangled with the motion of his cigarette, and other flashes of gold came from two rings, his watch and one of his incisors.

'I'd still do her, though. I mean, if I had to, I'd give her one,' Ryshkov proclaimed. 'Only problem is, she's Lillepuu's sister. I wouldn't lay a finger on her. I wouldn't even touch his sister's best mate.'

'Don't mock my client. You've put on weight, Genya,' I said, teasing my employer like an elder brother. 'You must have either a good memory or a vivid imagination to talk about getting laid. Or do you test your goods first? Get the lay of the land, if you know what I mean? You certainly don't get any for free…'

Ryshkov smoked quietly, then stood up and walked towards me, stretching like a hundred-kilo cat. Only the purr was missing. His belly sagged over his belt; he was the sort of fellow who had eaten whatever he pleased as a young man, but now, in middle age, his stomach protruded outwards – though the rest of his body was relatively slender.

He approached me and stared at me with his deep, black, perpetually dark eyes. I was worried I might have miscalculated his tolerance for a spot of humour. You never really knew what kind of mood Ryshkov was in. He always spoke in the same monotonous way, three words at a time, his face fixed in a single expression.

'Then I'll stop screwing them altogether – if I can't get any on the free market,' he scoffed, talkative by his own standards. He stubbed out his cigarette and lifted his smart suede jacket, then yawned. A bluish tinge of stubble peppered his cheeks. I'd never seen him looking energetic.

I did a lot of work for Ryshkov. I drove cars from Helsinki to Vyborg and St Petersburg, brought women to work in Finland, rented apartments and acquired goods for his various companies. I was always paid on time, and Ryshkov always kept his word. But I never understood what made him tick. I couldn't quite trust him.

Perhaps 'trust' sounds too grand. Even a crook can be trustworthy when you get to know him and reckon with his shortcomings. All I knew about Ryshkov was that he came from Moscow, never talked about his parents, couldn't remember his siblings or his home, never mentioned his school or his time in the army. I'd tried to ask, but he never offered any kind of explanation. I didn't really know what he thought of my nosy questions – or of me, for that matter. Now I got the feeling he was thinking about the disappearance of Sirje Lillepuu and drawing his conclusions.

'It's been the same for the last twenty years.' When he realized I hadn't quite understood, he added: 'My weight.' He shook my hand as he left, and said he needed to pop into one of his restaurants downtown before heading off for the border crossing at Vaalimaa, then on to St Petersburg. I didn't ask what he was going for.

Ryshkov stopped at the door and turned towards me. He was playing with his car keys, letting them glide between his fingers, dangling the Mercedes star insignia on its golden chain like a cross on a rosary.

'Listen up, country boy. Be bloody careful. I've had my disagreements with Jaak Lillepuu, but we've sorted them out. It was a heavy case, pretty nasty too. Lillepuu is in a different league from your Karelian pimps and drunken petty criminals.'

I couldn't remember Ryshkov ever warning me of anything before.

3

I turned the sign hanging from a chain on the door and locked the office. In my absence, the sign asked clients to call me and gave my mobile-phone number. I walked across to the corner of the market and went down into the metro station.

Ryshkov had been keen for me to take care of a small bit of business for him. It seemed harmless enough, but perhaps that was why it was making me nervous. I was to fetch a bag from a luggage locker and take it to an address in Töölö. I didn't ask why he couldn't take it himself.

I took the metro to the Central Railway Station, winding my way through the underpass and trying not to make eye contact with the junkies and gangs of Somali youths; then I took the escalator up to the arrivals hall. A group of young men loitered by the kiosk on the corner. They looked at me a fraction too long, then guiltily glanced away. I recognized at least three Ingrian boys among them.

The boys' relatives had opened up about their suspicions of mobile-phone theft, pickpocketing, drug dealing and getting into fights. I could see the boys' sagging trousers were top-of-the-range, and their snowboarding bags were high-end and exclusive; their uncomfortable-looking shoes were too expensive, and their mobiles too small. It was all too much, given what I knew of their parents' jobs, salaries and state benefits.

I tried to steer well clear of the mess; this was no time to start playing social worker. I looked right past the boys' stares; I didn't nod at them and didn't raise a hand, just headed for the luggage lockers. I handed over the ticket I'd been given and was presented with a black bag with the name DIADORA emblazoned on its side. I slung the bag over my shoulder as if it were my own, walked between the Post Office and the Sokos department store and headed for the tram stop.

I waited for almost ten minutes, trying to look like an average-sized, averagely well-dressed man carrying an average-looking sports bag. The number three rattled to a halt, and I bought a single ticket. I knew it would have been cheaper to get a ten-journey ticket, but I didn't want to carry anything around in my pockets that could reveal all my comings and goings. I stood right at the back of the tram, rode past the Olympic Stadium and stepped off as the dual-language announcement came for Sallinkatu–Salligatan.

There was a key in the bag's side pocket. I unlocked the iron gate out front and stepped into the courtyard, then from there into the stairwell. I walked up to the first-floor landing and waited there. It was quiet, dim and hot. I waited first three minutes, then another three. Nobody had followed me inside. I took the lift up to the sixth floor and walked back down to the fifth. The name on the door was 'Kyllönen', and beneath that was a sticker that read: NO ADVERTISEMENTS. I rang the doorbell, but nobody opened the door: nobody was supposed to. I unlocked the door. The one-room apartment was small and uninhabited but neatly furnished. I peered into the fridge and bathroom: both were warm and empty.

I left the bag on the sofa bed, and the keys on the draining board in the kitchenette. I had no idea what was in the bag, and I didn't want to know. It might have contained anything from steroids for distribution around the city's gyms, red knickers and dildos or made-to-order passports, for all I knew. Ryshkov had sworn flippantly on his mother's life that the bag didn't contain drugs or human limbs, and that was good enough for me. I had no problem carrying the less serious stuff.

The ring of my mobile phone startled me. RUUSKANEN CALLING, flashed the screen. Ruuskanen ran a car dealership by the ring road on the outskirts of the city. He had a Russian buyer for a tax-free Mercedes, and he needed an interpreter and someone to fill in the paperwork. We agreed on a time and hung up. I gave the apartment the once over, peered into the corridor through the peephole to check the stairwell was still empty, and left.

I didn't go back along Mannerheimintie, but strolled down the street towards Urheilukatu and walked to the Olympic Stadium. Construction work was underway on a new football stadium on a strip of land that had once been an old ballpark. I stopped to look at the site. A group of pensioners had congregated by the fence to bemoan the achievements of modern architecture.

Inside the Olympic Stadium a security guard the size of a sumo wrestler was slouching in a chair inside the glass entrance booth and deigned to wave me through when I told him I was only going to talk to a friend and wasn't planning on paying the 10-euro entrance fee for the privilege. I instantly regretted it. I should have simply plodded in casually instead of drawing attention to myself with explanations, and answered only if he'd asked me directly what I thought I was doing.

A seemingly endless game was in progress on the volleyball court; at the end of the basketball court, a couple of kids were dummying past a succession of virtual opponents, and on the upper level the boxers and table-tennis players were sweating away as they worked out. The Olympic Stadium always made me feel good. The building itself, its sounds and smells, gave the promise of post-exercise intoxication, just as a liquor store promised a good fix for an alcoholic. In truth, the place reminded me of former days at the courts and halls of the sports academy in Leningrad. Sunlight heralding the arrival of spring glinted in the high-set windows, and the white of the walls intensified the brightness; across the open space, young girls practised their gymnastics programmes in time to imagined music, and the clatter of the weight machines rang throughout the hall, the sound gaining fresh momentum as it echoed off the walls.

Anatoly Stepashin was lifting weights on the bench. I waited quietly. Anatoly stood up, dried his face and draped a towel around his neck. He shook my hand but didn't say anything – he merely gulped water from his bottle. I took a step away from the bench, and Stepashin followed me. A tattooed man in tracksuit bottoms began a new set in his place.

'You're certainly all talk today, Tolya,' I smiled at him. I was able to see the top of Stepashin's head. His black hair was sprouting upwards like a hedgehog's spikes. Stepashin said nothing, and he didn't smile back.

'Listen, straight up, I need some information. How well do you know Jaak Lillepuu and, more to the point, do you know anything about his sister, Sirje Lillepuu? Kosher, in her early thirties, no funny business, married to a Finnish guy called Larsson.'

I spoke quietly in Russian, but tried to pronounce the names carefully. Stepashin took another gulp from his water bottle and watched one of the gymnastics girls executing her floor routine. She overextended on a series of somersaults, and Stepashin's shoulders tensed in empathy as she came crashing to her knees.

I knew Anatoly from my time in Leningrad. He had once been a decent gymnast, taken his diploma at the academy and then toured with the circus all the way from Minsk to Ulan Bator, from Kishinev to Omsk. He had travelled with acrobats, magicians, trapeze artists, bears and dogs right across the Soviet Union. He had stood in the sawdust, the sturdy foundation of a human pyramid, his face hidden behind a mask, though his sad face needed no clown make-up whatsoever.

In Finland, he worked in business that was almost legitimate. At Ryshkov's gyms he drew up workout routines and led exercise and acrobatics classes for theatre students. Anatoly was originally one of the Russian diaspora living in Tallinn. As a student, he had spoken only a few words of Estonian or Finnish. Three years in Helsinki had changed things. And I knew he had contact with the Estonians in Helsinki.

'Jaak Lillepuu? He's a bad man,' Anatoly said soberly. He looked me directly in the eyes and repeated the words in Finnish. 'A very bad man! But I don't know his sister. I've seen her once or twice, but I don't think she's got anything to do with Jaak's business dealings. Still, once a mummy's boy, always a mummy's boy. Jaak went off on his own when he was young. He did time inside back in the Soviet days.'

I showed Anatoly the photograph of Sirje.

'Yep, that looks like her. But like I said, I don't know anything about her. Why are you interested?'

'She's gone missing; her husband doesn't know where she is. I'm just trying to find her.'

'Well, I can ask around. But don't hold your breath. I'll have to be careful who I ask.'

I thanked him and started walking towards the exit and the tram stop outside. Though I might not get anything useful out of Anatoly Stepashin, word was out around town now that I was looking for Sirje Larsson – Sirje Lillepuu.

That night I had a dream.

I am at home in Sortavala. It's the afternoon. I am standing in front of the radio. Its polished wood surfaces are gleaming, and lights and the names of cities glow in the front glass panel, the tubes and reels giving off warmth and a smell unlike that of any other appliance we have. The sun lights a spot on the rug and dust hangs in the air. Mother sits in the rocking chair, swinging gently back and forth, a book in her lap. I've just come back from school, that much I know; my satchel is on the floor and I am wearing my Pioneer scarf. Father walks in. He's wearing a greenish uniform. My fingers remember the shapes of the badges on his chest and the thick material of his military uniform, the cigarettes in his pocket. This time he doesn't hug me: You're a big boy now. *Without taking off his officer's cap, he tells Mother to follow him, commanding her in a voice that I can't recall. 'Father, no, no,' I shout, panicked. The dead can't shout out orders, I try to tell myself, and Mother turns to look at me. She wears a pair of dark sunglasses, like a blind woman in an old film.*

I woke up and stared at the ceiling. 'Decorator's White, colour code F-157,' I repeated to myself, until I was able to fully grasp reality – until I understood where I was. The red digits on the clock radio read 04:55. Had the sound of the newspaper delivery woken me up? It was still dark. Hakaniemi hummed with the sounds of the waking city. I turned onto my side, pressed the pillow against my ear and tried to convince myself: *You can sleep for another three hours. You can sleep for another three hours.*

I knew I'd eventually drift off to sleep, but I kept jolting awake. I recalled the images from my dream, Mother in her dark sunglasses. I wished I weren't sleeping alone.

4

I'd asked Larsson if I could inspect Sirje's belongings. I looked among the papers he'd given me to find a direct telephone number for the bookstore. 'Larsson's Collectible Books,' he answered after half a ring tone. We agreed I'd pay him a visit around six that evening.

By ten to six I was looking for the building in what was called the 'dollar end' of Pakila. I remembered that the other side of the neighbourhood was considered less affluent, and was referred to as the 'rouble zone'. To my mind, both halves were identical strongholds of the Finnish middle classes: ridge-roofed wooden houses built after the war, houses later extended with glass conservatories, lavish gardens, complex brick constructions, and terraced houses all crammed alongside one another.

The driveway up to Larsson's house rose from street level and led into a small front garden. I had left the office in my own car, an old brown Volvo 240 with a good twenty years' service to its credit, the kind of car you would expect to be driven by a neatly dressed old gent, his wife sitting by his side in a fur coat.

All I wanted was a car that worked, and didn't draw too much attention to itself. I'd bought it from Ruuskanen, who had praised the Volvo's fuel-injection engine. 'This beauty moves like a pike.'

I wasn't much of a fisherman, but I imagined that meant the car accelerated nicely. I insulted the Volvo just enough, haggled him down, agreed a price and rounded off by reminding him of the Ministry of Transport inspectors in Petroskoi who didn't use their screwdrivers on the chassis, but went straight for the car dealer's bodywork. Ruuskanen assured me he'd understood the importance of a fully comprehensive insurance package. I've been happy with my investment ever since.

I drove through the open gate, steered the car into the garden and parked by the front steps, though I could see that the path and tire tracks continued beyond the house. I guessed the garage must have been at the bottom of the incline near the entrance to the basement level. The snow on the drive and pathway had been neatly shovelled away; the shapes and corners of the snow verges wouldn't have been out of place in a geometry textbook. Larsson had heard my arrival. He was waiting at the door.

Every house, every home, has its own smell. The smell of Larsson's house was cool, a sharp note of lemon, perhaps from parquet wax or detergent, a hint of pipe tobacco and the acrid odour of newly lacquered furniture or silicon from a recent bathroom renovation. I committed these smells to memory. Did I really think that, once I found Sirje, I would be able to confirm her identity by smell?

Larsson gave me a quick tour of the house, promised to help me or give me advice whenever necessary and left me alone in the living room, saying he would carry on with his chores in the basement workshop. I assured him I would look around calmly, carefully but thoroughly, and said I respected his trust.

I examined the living room quickly. Uncomfortable-looking furniture, which I guessed was Gustavian in style; a set of coffee tables featuring a chessboard; a box of cigarettes full of dried Marlboros; an ashtray; empty vases. The walls bore cheerless paintings: frigid Finnish landscapes and two faded floral still-lifes. I lifted the lid from the piano keyboard and played the old time signal from Radio Moscow with the fingers of one hand.

'*Not a leaf moves in the forest…*' Larsson's voice startled me. He had come back upstairs unnoticed, and was standing at the living-room door. I changed the melody to *The Lights of Moscow*.

'The guy who composed that song was a real Stalinist bloodhound, you know… The piano isn't really in tune.'

'Maybe, I don't know. I mean, I don't know about Tikhon Khrennikov; but the piano's fine.' I tried to sound indifferent, but Larsson was already making his way from the hallway down to the basement with a briefcase in his hand.

In addition to the living room and hallway, the ground floor had a kitchen, a tidy fusion of old-fashioned space, tiles, cupboards and modern appliances. Behind the kitchen was a small room, perhaps once reserved for servants. It had its own small bathroom and a separate entrance. The room had been redesigned and turned into a guest room, though beneath the bedspread there were no sheets. The cupboards were bare save for one, which had a year's worth of women's magazines on its bottom shelf. I looked at the labels: they were all addressed to Sirje Larsson. The shelves had been carefully lined with yellow floral protective paper. In the bathroom, I turned on the tap; it gurgled for a moment, then spat out a gush of rusty water. Overnight guests were clearly a rare event in this household.

There was another wooden door in the living room. I opened it, and from the smell I knew this must be Aarne Larsson's office. The walls were covered in bookshelves. On the desk were a run-of-the-mill laptop, a writing pad and a pencil case. The desk chair was a more modern, office model, and on the floor beside it was a pair of black leather slippers. The room was dim, because the window faced the morning sun. The view outside was neat and dozy, like a Sunday afternoon in a small town. You could imagine couples out for a walk in matching tracksuits, curtains drawn across the windows so that the sunlight didn't disturb anyone watching a film or a Formula One race.

I looked upwards. In the middle of the white panelled ceiling was a two-propeller model aircraft hanging by its navel. It was fashioned from beautiful layers of wood. It gleamed, dark-brown and varnished, and right in the middle was a neat, undecorated insignia: a blue swastika inside a white circle.

I am a product of Soviet society, and certain things have been taught and explained to me in such a way that they produce a reflex like the blow of a doctor's hammer against the kneecap. The Nazi symbol startled me; I took a step back, though I realized that the symbol on the aircraft was the wartime insignia of the Finnish air force and not that of the Third Reich.

I'm not an expert in war history or aviation, so I left the aircraft hanging in the air and began inspecting Larsson's bookshelves. The selection of books didn't shock me, and now I understood that Larsson's interests were in line with the model aircraft. The library focused on political history, the Second World War, Germany and the Soviet Union. It was a stylistically pure collection of staunch reactionary literature, though I wasn't quite sure what such adjectives meant these days. And although shivers were running the length of my back like sparks of light hissing in a short-circuited meter, I was sure the books and the swastika had nothing to do with Sirje's disappearance.

I moved upstairs. The upper hallway opened up into a second living room with a standard, light-coloured three-piece suite (I couldn't say whether it was from Ikea or Asko), a television, a stereo and shelves of CDs and vinyl records, a few metres of fiction and a couple of modernist paintings on the walls.

The furniture in the couple's bedroom was white and modern, the wallpaper a light bluish grey. I imagined the occupants sleeping there, cool and light; there was nothing dark about this room, though it was directly above the foreboding office downstairs.

On the dressing table were a few of Sirje Larsson's effects: combs, a hairbrush, a few lipsticks and mascara brushes, a hairband or two. The drawer contained more make-up, sanitary towels and tampons, a hairdryer, newspapers and small bottles of shampoo and soaps that she had picked up at various hotels.

Next to the telephone on the table was an oblong diary, its pages containing only a few entries. Aarne Larsson went to a meeting a few times a week. In a small, round hand the words 'Sirje's aerobics' appeared once a week, as well as the regular entry 'Painting' every Tuesday evening at 6.00 PM. The empty rows and the margins had been decorated with doodles of flowers, dogs and horses.

There were no telephone numbers in the diary, no meetings with friends. It wasn't enough to put together the jigsaw puzzle of a missing life.

Larsson was sitting on a tall stool, hunched, devotedly sewing up the leather cover of an old book. The basement featured a battered, stainless-steel worktop, a washing machine, ironing equipment and a clothes press; a chest freezer, archive folders and magazines were lined up neatly on the shelves. I glanced at the effects and politely followed Larsson's work, but couldn't think of anything pertinent to say.

'You visited the office,' Larsson said, saving us from the silence. His forehead indicated the upstairs room, but he didn't look at me. 'I'm interested in history, the Finnish kindred peoples and so on. Some seemed surprised, and in the past people used to mock me, but you must surely understand, given you yourself once lived under the yoke of the Soviet Union. And yet you're not remotely Russian, that much I know about you.'

These were the longest sentences I'd heard Larsson say.

'Yes...' I replied, still trying to sound neutral, and glanced around the basement. I opened the cupboard doors and peered into the cold sauna. The basement also housed a boiler room and a garage. Larsson owned a metallic grey Saab 9000.

'I haven't come up with any new information about Sirje yet – no friends' telephone numbers, no Post-it notes. I understand she takes painting classes somewhere?'

'Yes; a course at the adult-education centre. She enjoys oil painting. I don't know how many courses she's taken. She has something of a bent for that sort of thing.

'She has a number of... artistic friends,' Larsson continued. 'But other than that, she doesn't have friends here. She travels to Tallinn quite often to visit her family, a few times a month. Of course, I have nothing against that, absolutely not.'

Larsson's voice hardened, and he looked up at me from behind his brown-rimmed spectacles. Back at the office he had been wearing a pair of glasses with metal frames; these were probably an old pair, demoted to use in the basement.

'I assume you'll also have to ask whether Sirje had any enemies. For the life of me, I can't think of any. We once received a threatening letter – anonymous, of course – calling her an "Estonian whore" and me a "dirty old man", but that was a while ago now, and it surely can't have anything to do with Sirje's disappearance. One of our barmy neighbours, I imagine, or someone with an axe to grind about ethnic Finnish purity.'

'Do you still have the letter?'

'No,' said Larsson gently, with a slight shake of the head. 'It was in a standard white envelope, typed up, no signature. We threw it away.'

I thanked him for his help, shook his hand and reversed the Volvo into the street. I drove a few hundred metres from the house and walked back, leaned against a lamppost and watched the street's dormant life. If I'd been a smoker, I'd have lit a cigarette. The lights in Larsson's house glowed steadily; a black Audi reversed into the street from the neighbour's front garden and accelerated off towards the Tuusulantie highway; but apart from that, the number of events totalled zero.

I tried to assess Larsson's neighbours. His house was on the corner; on the plot opposite was a small two-storey terrace, but the next building up the hill was semi-detached, with the entrance to the first apartment opening towards the Larssons'.

I approached the oak-veneered door and rang the bell. There came a distant *ding-dong* and the bark of a dog. A fair-haired woman in her forties opened the door. She wore a pair of jeans, a hoodie and cloying perfume, and was barefoot; I could see the dark-red of her toenails.

'Good evening. Jari Kesonen, from Jurista,' I introduced myself. 'I'm investigating a case in the neighbourhood, and wondered if I could ask you a few questions.' I showed the woman a laminated photo ID card that proved that I was indeed a Mr Jari Kesonen, head researcher at Jurista Legal Services.

The firm certainly existed, and it owned properties and vehicles across the city, but it didn't take on any legal jobs – at most, it created them. Its business matters were effectively handled via Gennady Ryshkov's desk. I'd made the card myself.

Marjatta Nyqvist wasn't much help. She listened to my spiel with a pleasant smile, invited me inside and sat me down on a beige sofa with sharp, geometrical corners. I explained the gist of matters truthfully. The only factually incorrect parts were my name and that of the company I claimed to represent, but I've realized that even a bogus Finnish lawyer makes a much better impression than a bona fide Karelian immigrant investigator. I'd tried to achieve the same impression with my appearance, too; I put great effort into looking effortlessly well-dressed. In fact, it was Ryshkov who took care of my wardrobe. He ordered relatively high-end copies of designer suits at a factory in Käkisalmi, just across the border, and sometimes I bought or otherwise acquired prototypes of original Italian-model suits.

I nattered away. My hostess smiled at me, and over the course of our conversation she began to look rather attractive – though at first I'd thought she was a bit past her sell-by date. I tried to work out when I'd last been with a woman. I looked at the curve of her neck, and imagined how my stubble would tickle it; I would inhale her smell and listen to her sighs, her purrs…

Marjatta Nyqvist said something that I didn't hear, and I grunted to indicate I agreed. I knew she had noticed my gaze, and she didn't seem to frown on it. She smiled – either with motherly understanding or girlish seductiveness.

'I didn't know her very well,' she said, bringing us both back to the matter of Sirje Larsson. 'We only ever said hello, really. In the summer we'd visit each other's gardens or chat across the hedge. She wasn't very talkative or sociable, but she was friendly enough; there was no bad blood between us. We just didn't have much to do with one another.'

The Nyqvists had lived in Pakila for a good ten years and knew the neighbourhood well. Marjatta guessed Sirje Larsson didn't have many friends in the area. The Larssons kept to themselves, and nobody appeared to have a grudge against them.

'I'd say they seemed a very… *stable* couple, happy even, if anyone can ever be really happy,' Marjatta ventured. I imagined I saw a brief flash in her eyes, a glint of longing.

I wondered what she would look like naked, standing there soft and fair, slightly heavier than a young girl, her round breasts full, already sagging slightly. She'd shake her hair as if to demonstrate that a grown woman has nothing to be ashamed of, that she was at home in her own skin. But Marjatta Nyqvist was still in front of me in her jeans and overpowering perfume, smiling at me the way a knowing woman smiles. I stammered a thank-you and said I might have to bother her at a later date.

'Sure,' she answered breezily, and pressed the door shut.

I went back to the car and pulled up in front of Larsson's and Nyqvist's houses. For a while I sat there in the darkness, thinking things over. After visiting her home, I was none the wiser about Sirje's disappearance. What did Sirje Larsson do during the daytime? What did she think, whom did she speak to? I tried to list all my possible questions.

I'd assumed I would establish Sirje's whereabouts with just a few questions, then simply find the runaway, bring her home and send Larsson the bill: ten grand plus tax and expenses. Now I was beginning to suspect the job wouldn't be that simple after all.

The lights in Larsson's house were still on. I couldn't make out any movement in the house. The neighbour's door opened, and Marjatta came bounding outside with surprisingly light steps and a brown setter excitedly jumping up and down at the end of a leash.

I steered my Volvo back towards Hakaniemi.

5

I was sitting in the office going through the paperwork for a shipment of pine snag that had come in from Suojärvi when Valery Karpov stepped inside. I was surprised, pleased even – and worried. Karpov didn't usually travel to Helsinki without letting us know he was coming. At the very least, he would have called us on the way, saying the star-emblazoned locomotive of the St Petersburg–Helsinki train had just passed Imatra and that I'd better reserve a table at a decent restaurant, because he'd be hungry when he arrived.

Karpov furrowed his brow and looked concerned, even more no-nonsense than usual. I remembered my dream, my mother in her dark sunglasses. I'd forgotten to call her. Again.

'Karpov, my man. What brings you to Helsinki? Nothing's happened in Sortavala, has it?'

'Not in Sortavala; on the Finnish side. Some wanker has emptied the fucking warehouse, cleaned out the booze, all the bloody cigarettes. Shit, man, that stuff was worth at least a million marks.'

I was amused at Karpov's rage, but I kept my smile in check, because my friend certainly wasn't in the mood for humour. We'd met one another as schoolboys at a pan-Soviet ski camp in Kaukolovo. We'd skied hundreds of kilometres together; by sharing the same bottle, we'd both learned how to drink liquor, and we'd kept in touch when we were studying in Leningrad. Valery was of Karelian extraction; he spoke pitch-perfect Finnish and looked like the chiselled embodiment of Finnish purity. He'd ended up becoming a telephone engineer.

Or rather, he became a businessman. Valery stopped dabbling in telecommunications around the time of the 'Gorbachev' mobile phone. Nowadays he sold birch firewood and coloured scrap metal to the West, shipped washing machines and electric stoves to the East, oversaw the flow of illegal liquor and tobacco along the road between Sortavala and Värtsilä and was, apparently, seeking to 'develop the infrastructure of tourism in Valamo', as I'd recently read in the *Karjalainen* newspaper. In plain Russian, that meant taking control of all the ferries, kiosks and restaurants used by the tourists so that, for every rouble spent, plenty of kopeks came jangling into Karpov's coffers.

In Finland, Karpov and Gennady Ryshkov were business partners, or at least they had agreed on a division of labour. This suited me fine, as I worked for both of them. But now they had common cause for concern.

'That shipment was bound for Helsinki. Gennady's fucking furious. And so am I; we've both got a hell of a lot of money riding on this,' Karpov frothed.

The goods had been taken across the border in small quantities and stored in a corrugated-iron warehouse in Kesälahti. 'Some wanker' had driven a truck into the warehouse forecourt, cut the locks with a blowtorch and taken the cardboard boxes full of bottles and cigarette cartons.

'Get the word out. The smokes are easy to spot; there's a spelling mistake on the box,' Karpov explained, a little embarrassed. 'It was my nephew's fault; he designed the template on his computer.' As evidence, Karpov produced a model packet. 'You see, it says "Marlboro" on the lid and "Fine Selected Tobacos" on the side? There's a C missing.'

He took out a cigarette and lit up, as if to demonstrate that his knock-off tobacco was good enough for a con artist like him, too. I decided that, at a more opportune moment, I should ask whether Valery was related to the Rettig entrepreneurs of Sortavala or the Philip Morrises of Käkisalmi. For now, it seemed wiser to keep my jokes to myself. Karpov inhaled hungrily on the cigarette, becoming increasingly animated as he recalled how events had unfolded.

'There was a guy called Yura Koshlov on guard at the warehouse. He was keeping his head down in the office. He's disappeared too, nothing left but a Thermos flask on the table full of hot water. I don't think Yura was involved in this; he's been working for me for a long time. Not the sharpest tool in the box. I think they've taken him out. God rest his soul.'

He crossed himself, cigarette in his fingers, but still managed to look respectful.

Karpov went into town on business and whinged about driving back to Sortavala that evening, though I had invited him to stay. Karpov was the kind of guy who could only remain serious and angry for about fifteen minutes, and even that was pushing it. As he left he even reminded us to apply for state funding for our upcoming IT project. This was his standard joke, which he repeated whenever we came across the ruins of an old collective barn driving around the Karelian outback: 'We'll turn this place into a technology park, boys, okay?'

I decided to potter around the office as long as possible, but couldn't seem to get anything done. I tried to call my mother a few times, but she didn't answer. The telephone lines in Karelia were occasionally on the blink, but this time the ringtone sounded functional. I imagined the old phone rattling in my mother's kitchen, or the scullery as we used to call it, on the small table in front of the window. There were probably geraniums on the windowsill, patterns embroidered in red and blue on the white tablecloth.

Mother still didn't pick up. Maybe she was visiting the neighbours or helping one of the less mobile elderly people in the village, I thought.

I called around and asked about Sirje Larsson, but my network of contacts still didn't seem to know anything about her. At around eight o'clock I locked up the office and walked once round the block, as I did every evening. I couldn't see anyone following me, so I walked into the courtyard and from there into the stairwell. I lived in the same building as the office. From the room at the back you could go straight into the B stairwell, and from there via the basement or the courtyard to the A stairwell.

I lived on the upper floor, the seventh, and I liked my apartment. The building was peaceful. Most of the residents were retired working-class folk, their apartments small and cheap. I paid the rent for my office to Ryshkov, but my apartment was owned by a retired Helsinki couple who had invested their savings in studios and one-bedroom apartments for the rental market.

I read an English textbook, watched the news and the sports results and put on my running clothes. I hadn't been to the gym or done any exercise for a few days, and I felt the need to sweat. I headed for the road along the sea at Sörnäinen, warmed up with interval and coordination exercises, then ramped up the pace and jogged past the mountains of coal at the power plant and on towards Kalasatama. I ran almost as far as the Arabia neighbourhood; my route took me round the pallid structure of the city prison. I returned home through Vallila.

I didn't particularly enjoy running. It had always felt like a chore, even on the soft pathways winding through the light summer evenings in Karelia. I much preferred playing football or ice hockey a few times a week with my Russian friends; in the winter I'd go skiing. There had been precious little snow this year – I'd been out skiing maybe half a dozen times, and a few of those had been on work gigs further north in Lahti.

The shadowy pavements were slippery in places, but I managed to get home without falling over. I looked for an even spot on the ground and did a set of one hundred jump squats. I wondered whether or not passers-by might find this amusing, thinking of me as an elderly fitness freak who scrupulously notes down every jump set in a small jotter and ends up tearing his Achilles tendon in the summer's only running competition, hobbling around afterwards with his ankle in plaster, proud of himself, only to return to the track the following year every bit as pitifully keen.

Once back home I had a shower, brewed some tea, ate a round of sandwiches and read a book about the Battle of Kollaa during the Winter War. Larsson would have approved, I mused.

6

I fell asleep and started dreaming.

I am in Sortavala again, at home, in my room. Mother is sitting on the bed saying something, and she turns to look at me. She's wearing the dark glasses again, and I can't see her eyes. A moment later I'm in the garden in front of the house; there's a light-blue Volga parked outside, and Aarne Larsson is standing there in grey 1960s summer attire with a bottle and some flowers in his hand. Sirje Larsson and Marjatta Nyqvist climb out of the back seat; I recognize the smell of the Volga's interior; I'm inside the car, looking at the dashboard from the back seat, and Aarne Larsson boasts that the steering wheel is made of ivory. The women explain that they have come for a funeral: 'Sorry we haven't dressed for the occasion.' They are dressed like the women in that Finnish–Swedish film I've seen. Wonderful Women by the Water, *I try to shout, and to Larsson I insist that it was our neighbour Maxim Semyonovich who tried to convince me his car's steering wheel was made of genuine ivory, not Larsson, and that the car was a Moskvitch and had a radio and a good heating system and that you could start it with the palm of your hand... I know everything everyone is saying, though the whole dream is silent; the others can't hear my shouting, but come rushing inside...*

I woke up and realized that I wasn't alone in the room. I kept my eyes closed and tried to continue breathing steadily, sleepily, listening to the sound breaking the silence in the room. The smell of outdoor clothes, tobacco and grilled food hung in the air. I tried to identify where my guest was.

'Morning, Kärppä. I know you're awake. Your ears are twitching.'

I opened my eyes and sat up, leaning against the headboard.

'Korhonen. Good morning. Here I am wondering who broke into my apartment, but it was the police all along. Did I leave my keys in the door, or did Parjanne help you take it off the hinges?'

I was genuinely relieved. The police were the kind of night-time guests I was least worried about. I was constantly expecting to have a pistol aimed at my head or to be beaten up at any moment. For burglars, my apartment offered only slim pickings.

I continued: 'I suppose it's one way to keep you off the streets, and you know I love a good chinwag, but might I ask what you boys are up to?'

Korhonen was a criminal investigator a few years older than me. I bumped into him regularly – or rather, he bumped into me when it suited him. Korhonen liked to keep up with goings-on in the Russian underworld, and a few times I'd explained to him how people and business worked on our side of the border. I think he assumed I wanted to keep things just within the letter of the law; he left me in peace as long as I didn't try and pull a fast one on him.

Wearing a jacket way too smart to belong to a policeman, Korhonen sat down in the chair at the end of my bed to eat his kebab. He tore the paper wrapping open and chomped loudly, taking care not to dirty the blue wool of his sleeves or his yellow scarf. Parjanne stood behind him, arms folded. He was a detective inspector, and often accompanied Korhonen. He wore a waist-length leather jacket and his hair was cropped short.

I took my watch from the bedside table. It was half past four. 'Well, I would have got up in a good three and a half hours anyway,' I said in a deadpan voice.

'Don't play lord of the manor. We were driving past and thought we'd pay you a visit,' said Korhonen. 'We saw the lights on in a kebab place over in Kallio, and the boys kindly made us some supper. We asked if there was any hash around, but they assured me they were just hanging out. What was it, stocktaking, spring cleaning, Ali Baba's birthday or something? And you know the Kebab Brothers' names, Kärppä? Shish, Döner and Falafel, of course!' Korhonen rolled off the names without a hint of irony. 'Parjanne here didn't care for one. He's a vegan.'

'For the love of Christ...' Parjanne sighed wearily.

'No, we're not interested in Christ. But have you heard of a Yura Koshlov? He's a skiing man like yourself, and from the same neck of the woods, too. Well, he'll have no use for his skis now. We found Koshlov this morning in the boot of a Primera parked outside a supermarket in Malmi. These Japanese cars have got so little storage space, they'd chopped him up so he'd fit in better.' Korhonen's voice was a low hiss. He barely opened his mouth at all; the voice seemed to escape from between his stiff jaws.

'And I've got a bad feeling you know something about this little scenario,' Korhonen spat. 'Let's see if I can help you: your mates Ryshkov and Karpov had a bit of a falling out, and poor Yura ended up dead by accident.'

'No, that's not how it is,' I tried to shrug the matter off.

'Well how is it, then? Start talking,' he said.

I looked first at Korhonen, then at Parjanne.

'Hey, Parjanne, why don't you go and see a man about that anaconda of yours, eh?' said Korhonen. 'Bathroom,' he added when Parjanne didn't seem to understand. 'No, I know, why don't you go and check if I'm still in the car?'

Parjanne sighed more heavily than usual, his expression impassive, and walked outside.

'I don't much like your friend. He turned my office upside down once, though he knew I had nothing to do with the case,' I said.

'I'll tell you what'll be upside down, and it won't be your office,' said Korhonen. 'Now stop whinging like a girl and tell me about Koshlov.' Then he added: 'He's not all that mean, our Parjanne. He's just a bit simple. His favourite actor is Also Starring, and his favourite food, the appetizers. See, now you've got me started again! Stop pissing about and tell me about Koshlov.'

I told him that Yura Koshlov did odd jobs for Karpov, that Karpov had a shipment of goods stolen and that Yura had disappeared along with it. I repeated myself, emphasizing the point that Ryshkov had nothing whatsoever to do with this matter and that he and Karpov had no conflicting interests.

'I don't know who stole the stuff or who did the killing. But I have an interest in finding out. To put it bluntly and confidentially,' I rounded off.

Korhonen didn't have the patience to listen without interrupting. I knew he was smart, and that all the while he was mentally running my account against what he'd already heard elsewhere.

'Take a long walk off a very short pier, eh? Every time you swear confidentiality, I feel like shooting you in the foot.

Christ, you hang around with murderers, hookers and half of Chechnya, and you talk like you're Esa bleeding Saarinen – you know who that is, right? I'll give *you* "conflicting interests",' he aped me, trying to sound serious.

'Before long we'll have all kinds of crazies allocating resources and commissioning consultant reports on development management in skilled organizations. Staff are our most important resource... as we walk the path of darkness...' Korhonen let the words glide out, half singing, and rounded off with a final barb: 'For Christ's sake, it's always the same with you people. What's the stolen gear? What is it this time? Totem-poles from the woodwork class? Pull the other one! Semiconductors from Säkkijärvi? Silicon chips from Kontupohja?'

'I'll tell you what I know, but I won't lie. I think it was fairly harmless stuff – liquor and tobacco. No drugs or firearms.' Then I added: 'And he's a *philosopher*. Esa Saarinen. And I know his wife and twins, and his wife's ex-husband. I've studied women's magazines for years.'

Korhonen stood up, stretched and looked at his watch. It occurred to me that he looked like a retired sportsman. I'd just never asked what sport. In the hallway, he couldn't pass the mirror without stopping. With the edge of his hand, he pressed down his wavy hair and admired himself with exaggerated affection. At the doorway, he turned back once more.

'Ah yes, I almost forgot. What in Christ's name are you doing getting mixed up with the bloody Estonians for? Word has it you're looking into Lillepuu. Changing sides, are we? Or else what the hell's going on?'

7

The following morning, I felt the urge to work out again. I went to the Olympic Stadium and lifted weights for an hour and a half, stretched and did some callisthenics on the floor. I felt pumped and strong as I drove back to Kallio.

Juha Toropainen's café had started life as Toro, a bog-standard coffee-and-steak joint. Then its owner had started developing his business concept: new interior, new strippers every couple of weeks and private booths at the back of the building for one-on-one performances. I wasn't interested in a private erotic show, though the Estonian girls seemed game enough.

The afternoon ambiance in Sex-Toro was one of a sleepy morning. A cleaner mopped the floors; the outside doors were open, forcing fresh air into the space, and even the daylight, dazzling and flashing in from between the curtains, seemed like an unwanted guest from entirely the wrong place. The manager himself was standing behind the bar, counting rows of bottles, noting down amounts in a small jotter, and nodded a terse greeting at me in one of the mirrors. I sat down at the bar and waited.

'Well fuck me, Kärppä.' Toropainen turned and poured himself some water from a tap at the bar.

'Can't complain. Shouldn't you be pouring that water into bottles? I've heard a man can down six vodkas on the trot here without a care in the world, then drive himself home – and if he's caught, his breathalyser test only shows 0.2 milligrams.'

'Yep, and you Russians have discovered an amazing new hooch,' Toropainen countered. '"Liquor light", they call it – only 16 per cent... Listen, what doesn't vibrate and doesn't fit up your ass? A Russian ass-vibrator. Now enough of the small talk. What do you want?'

'I'm looking for an Estonian woman. She's not in the business, but I thought I'd ask your girls, see if they know anything.'

Toropainen beckoned me behind the bar and ushered me out through the back. Beside the swing doors in the kitchen there was a table, around which sat four young women. One was eating porridge; the others had mugs of coffee. The coffee drinkers smoked in silence. The table was covered in eggshells, margarine tubs scraped clean and crumpled napkins.

I introduced myself and told them what I was after. The smokers continued puffing away; the porridge-eater's spoon momentarily stopped in midair before she, too, continued enjoying her breakfast. None of them said anything. I told them my story again: 'I'm looking for a woman who's gone missing; her name is Sirje Larsson or Sirje Lillepuu. She's Jaak Lillepuu's sister. She's been living in Helsinki for years, but she's originally from Tallinn... Even the smallest piece of information could be helpful,' I implored them, and passed around her photograph.

The women remained stubbornly silent. Eventually one of them shrugged her shoulders. 'Doesn't look familiar.'

I offered them my card and asked them to call me if they heard anything about Sirje. The only thing they promised was a discount if I ever needed a massage. I smiled politely and left them to get themselves geared up for the evening shift at Sex-Toro.

'With a customer card, every fifth time is free,' the redheaded porridge-eater shouted after me. 'And that's not all: you can collect bonus points, too!'

'*Hea tagumik*,' I heard them laughing in Estonian. I imagined they were admiring the contours of my manly backside, and decided to reward them by walking with an exaggerated swing in my hips like a model on a catwalk. The women giggled.

I'd just returned to the office when the phone rang. An out-of-breath female voice spoke in stiff, clumsy Finnish.

'You was asking about woman... I might have seen her.'

I enquired further, but the Estonian girl either didn't know anything else or wouldn't tell me. She simply thought she might have seen Sirje Lillepuu in a block of flats in the Herttoniemi area of the city. She even provided me with an address. I thanked her for the information.

'You owe me now; I don't want nothing to do with this. I never told you this.' She hung up, leaving the beeping of the phone to continue her conversation.

That evening I drove to Siilitie, near Herttoniemi, and parked the car outside a small pub. A friendly-looking spitz was tethered to the bike rack by its leash. It looked as though it was guarding the solitary women's bike left there. The sign in the window promised pizza, karaoke, darts and billiards. I surmised that this was one establishment in which I would never spend an evening of my time.

I looked for the address given by Toropainen's dancing girl. The buildings were all seven- and eight-storey blocks, rising one after the other, and winding two- and three-storey houses built into the undulating rocky terrain. There were enough stairwells to get through the alphabet and almost two hundred house numbers.

Eventually I found the right house and doorway. The apartment was on the sixth floor; the surname on the door read 'Santanen'. The tidy corridor smelled of cooking and detergent.

I recalled the suburbs of Leningrad, the barracks that were home to thousands of people, with elevators smelling of piss, stairwells from which the lightbulbs had all been stolen, pieces of iron inexplicably sticking out of the floor, half-built concrete elements left in the yard next to the rusting climbing frames. I forced myself to remember how warm and soft it felt to be behind the soundproof door, sitting with people, eating and talking, being part of something.

I rang the bell; the apartment was silent. I went out into the yard and counted the windows in the storeys. Santanen's apartment was dark. Or whoever's apartment it was. 'Santanen' had clearly been allocated a city council house, but whether or not he was living there himself was another matter.

Council flats weren't supposed to be sublet, but people found ways of dodging the ban. The apartment might be home to a group of students, Hungarian air hostesses or a dozen Chinese-restaurant employees, though the official tenant would still be listed as 'Santanen'. Neighbours sometimes reported cases of illegal subletting, but subletting tenants who didn't cause any trouble were generally left in peace.

I leaned against a pine tree in the yard and watched the houses in the darkening evening. The stars grew brighter, as though someone were gradually turning up a dimmer switch; it was going to be a chilly spring evening. The blue glow of television screens flickered in sync in many of the windows as people watched the same channel.

Through the windows on the ground floor, I could see right inside. A stocky man with an earring and a ponytail tied tightly behind his head was ladling potatoes onto plates for his two little boys. The gravy was in a red pot; the mother lifted cartons of milk and doled out spoonfuls of grated carrot, an act that met with resistance from the children. Then she, too, sat down at the table. Pale light shone from a lamp dangling above the table, and the windowpane looked bluish-grey from the steam in the kitchen.

I thought of my own mother and recalled the meals we'd shared, just the two of us, after my father had died and Alexei had gone to Moscow to study, got married and decided to stay there. Mother and I would sit opposite each other, always in the same seats, eating potatoes with gravy and bread, vegetables and pickled cabbage. When I set off for Leningrad and decided to see the world, Mother was left alone at the table. I always followed the weather forecast for Karelia, and I knew it was a chilly spring evening in Sortavala today, only slightly drier; the same stars were in the sky, the same moon.

'What the hell are you doing here? Some kind of Peeping Tom?' A tense voice brought me back to Herttoniemi. I turned, but didn't fall back on the self-defence moves I'd learned in the army. Behind me was a woman around my mother's age. She stood staring at me, her mouth tightly pinched. She wore a dark granny hat and a grey, knee-length coat.

'I'm not peeping at anyone,' I assured her. 'The name's Jukka Pekkarinen, from the *Evening Reporter*.' I showed her the card I'd made, which bore the word PRESS. I'd scanned the logo for the newspaper and laminated my own photograph.

'I'm writing an article about the misuse of council properties. Someone is awarded an apartment, then they strike it rich and move elsewhere, but hold onto their council tenancy. Their kids move in and pay next to no rent, or they sublet the place and bank the profits.'

'Well, you hear rumours about that sort of thing,' the woman replied. 'If you ask me, you should be reporting on the state of these buildings. The council has only bothered renovating the F and H buildings, and all the others have been left to wrack and ruin. Can you believe it, there's a draught under the windows – you can stick your finger through the hole, it's so big! Sun shining through in the summer and snow blowing indoors in the winter... and to think of all those old folks paying a fortune out of their pensions...' She was getting into her stride.

I nodded at regular intervals and tried to look like I was listening, all the while keeping a keen eye on Santanen's windows. The old woman's speech had a metallic ring, and her S's hissed angrily. '...Worked hard all my life, I have.' She interrupted her monologue for a moment, dug a packet of cigarettes from her coat pocket and lit a Colt. Her smoking seemed out of place, but I didn't spend time thinking about it or the building's state of disrepair for much longer: the lights in Santanen's window had switched on.

I took the lift up to the sixth floor and rang the doorbell again. I was taken aback when the door was opened instantly. A puzzled-looking woman in her twenties stood in the doorway. She was wearing a black jumper, a loose, dark-grey pair of trousers and a few earrings. Her hair was red and tangled, and she looked at me inquisitively, like a small squirrel.

The woman was the same size as Sirje Larsson; she looked pleasant, attractive, but she wasn't Sirje Larsson. Bewildered, we stared at one another until we both started to laugh. She invited me inside.

That evening I went to sleep more content than I'd been for a long time. I had work lined up for the next few days and enough money in the bank to survive a couple of months without working at all if I wanted; and on top of that, my new female acquaintances brought a new element of excitement into my life.

I'd thought of Marjatta Nyqvist a few times and almost picked up the phone and called her, but I couldn't think of the best way to suggest a meeting. I guessed she might be interested in a little adventure, maybe even a bit more. I'd thought I could visit her house again and tell her who I really was. I imagined this would make me seem especially exciting. Marjatta would pretend to object; I would touch her gently, squeeze her just enough that she would know how desirable she was, and we would agree to take advantage of each other; we were adults with no ties or obligations that we were reluctant to break. Then, after a few months, the initial fervour would fade away, Marjatta would look mistily over my shoulder, squeeze out a couple of tears and say that she knows I never really wanted her, and her sobs would bring the relationship to an end.

But this Marja Takala was a far more interesting case. I'd introduced myself and told her what I was doing, and even given her a card with the correct name. Marja didn't seem startled, but told me quite plainly that she'd been living in the apartment for the past four months, paying rent to the anonymous Santanen, whom she had never met.

Santanen was subletting the apartment to students: in addition to Marja, the apartment was currently home to two girls studying at the school of economics. Marja told me she'd been at the university for five years studying 'psychology and that sort of thing'. The other girls were out and about, she said with a smile.

She had never heard of Sirje Larsson or any other Estonians; her two flatmates were from Veteli and Lappeenranta. I sat at the girls' kitchen table for an hour and learned that Marja Takala had a part-time job conducting telephone interviews for market-research companies. She was born in Jyväskylä, and had a mother, father and a little sister. When she was younger she had been into sprinting, and after graduating from high school she'd spent a year in Stockholm working at a home for the elderly.

Marja was talkative and open and pretty – and interested in me. She was inquisitive, and kept asking about me. We both smiled as I was about to leave and stood in the door trying to come up with something to say. The conversation had ended with a bland 'see you', but this time I planned on making sure we really did see each other again.

8

From the word 'go' the next morning, everything tasted sour. Aarne Larsson turned up at the office before nine. I didn't have much to tell him. Larsson listened to my rambling explanation of what I'd done so far, and paid me five grand in cash. I wrote him a receipt and marked the payment into the all-too-slender case file.

We agreed I would visit Tallinn.

'Though if I'm honest, I don't believe Sirje is there,' Larsson said. 'Her parents would have told me. They haven't seen her for a month, and they're extremely worried.'

He left for his bookshop, and I continued my desperate search. I trawled all the restaurants popular with the Estonian expat community, shops owned by local Estonians, any place any Estonian might once have visited. I asked about Sirje, showed people the photograph and tried to convince everyone I was looking into a relatively harmless disappearance. Many of them replied tersely. I assumed they thought I was Russian.

I tracked down a woman who had been in the same class as Sirje at high school and was now working in the men's clothing section of Stockmann's department store. I picked up two shirts; the woman measured my neck with a green tape measure, told me I was a 42 and chuckled as she told me the last time she'd seen Sirje was back in the days of the Soviet Union.

I was on my way out with my carrier bag when I heard a man's voice right up against the back of my head.

'Viktor Nikolayevich. I've bought a new recording of Rimsky-Korsakov's *Scheherazade*,' the soft baritone said in Russian. I was almost paralysed on the spot, but managed to continue out the door before stopping to rummage in my bag. I tried to look as though I'd lost something, tapped my pockets absentmindedly and found my keys in my jacket pocket.

I took my purchases to the car and sat down to think.

The man who had spoken into my ear had continued briskly on his way, speaking loudly to another man, then said goodbye and walked off along Keskuskatu towards the Central Railway Station. At the corner I saw him turn towards the shopping boulevard on Aleksanterinkatu. He was approximately my age, either of stocky build or a heavy bodybuilder, and dark-haired. I couldn't remember ever seeing him before, but I knew that every other man in Moscow looked like that. And I knew without a shadow of doubt that he'd been addressing me.

I had often smirked at code words, at the idea of someone coming up with them sitting at a battered desk in a dusty office where the high ceiling was dark and dirty, the air dry and rasping, the walls adorned with portraits of current leaders – photographs of old men that had been airbrushed so much they looked like painted cadavers, while next to the thick picture frames, burned into the wall by the sun, was the shadow of a photograph now removed, of bygone power. That someone, the lowest of the low-grade civil servants, nothing but a scribe, would conjure up codes and passwords and communicate them in an encrypted language that required them to be changed at irregular intervals, without knowing what the codes would be used for or who they were intended for or which of them would be used and which were only decoys.

The bureaucracy of secrecy had always amused me, but this time I wasn't laughing. The message – or, should I say, the order – was clear, and the code was simple. A composer and the name of a work, in the correct combination, meant 'come and meet me'. If, however, the voice had claimed that *Scheherazade* was a work by Mussorgsky, it would be a warning or a message to indicate that an agreed meeting would have to be cancelled. The masters of Russian music weren't my forte, but I'd studied them enough to know their works far better than the agents from the Finnish intelligence services. And that would have to be good enough.

I stepped out of my Volvo, put a few coins in the parking meter and walked down to Aleksanterinkatu. The meeting place was easy to locate using the old 'labyrinth rule': first right, left at the next corner, two turns to the right, then the same again if need be, until you realized you had reached your destination.

The man hadn't taken great pains to try and lose me. I turned right onto Aleksanterinkatu, then left onto Mikonkatu, at the corner of the Ateneum Art Museum I took a right up Yliopistonkatu, then turned right again onto Kluuvikatu. The man was waiting for me at the corner of Aleksanterinkatu. He was bareheaded; his suede jacket was unbuttoned, and he was wearing a pair of indoor shoes. He was cold.

We shook hands. 'Follow me. In the car,' he instructed, and raised a remote control towards a Mercedes parked on the yellow lines. The lights flashed and the door unlocked automatically.

'Diplomatic plates too; an embassy car. What kind of fucking amateur have they got tracking me?' I muttered in Finnish. 'We should have gone the whole hog and met up in a gay bar, that way we'd be even more certain to have someone on our tail.'

'Listen, Viktor, you're hardly a master yourself,' the man said. 'Looks to me as though things aren't really going your way, to put it mildly.'

The man wiped the condensation from his glasses and squinted at me. 'So I think I'll do just fine, don't you agree?' With this glib comment, he switched back to Russian. 'I imagine you've missed us. You must have thought we'd forgotten about you.'

I kept my mouth shut, though I knew I'd missed them about as much as the pictures of exotic STDs I'd secretly examined in our home medical book as a child.

'We'd like to ask you a little favour. It's a small job for which you will be compensated. You will receive a package in the post containing a number of microfilms. Take them to the community archives in Mikkeli and put them back in their rightful place.'

'Why?'

'Because we're asking you to,' said the man, and placed his metal-rimmed glasses on the bridge of his nose.

'We sometimes need new people – dead souls, if you will. The church records of the old Finnish parishes in Karelia are held at the community archives in Mikkeli. These records have been microfilmed, and nobody examines the originals any more. Sometimes we take people off the records, sometimes we put them back; we create grandfathers and grandmothers to give children parents and grandparents. You know how these things work, Viktor… Besides, your family and background were scrutinized too, when you moved back to Finland.'

'But my affairs are all in order. I've got bona fide paperwork to prove it,' I stammered.

The man smiled at me benevolently, as though I were a child. I almost expected him to start speaking louder and with exaggerated clarity. He continued in his pleasantly rounded voice:

'Correct, and correct. The truth is all about what things look like. We can always erase a few ancestors. As for the Russian paperwork on your father's side, it's even easier, as easy as performing a magic trick for children.'

The man clicked his fingers and looked me straight in the eyes. 'Abracadabra! I'm sure the Finnish authorities would be interested to hear all about your background, your education and your previous… associations.' The man spoke evenly; he could have been talking about the weather. 'They would probably make an example of you to warn any others, deport you back to Russia.'

We sat there in silence. The windows steamed up. The man revved the ignition and turned on the heater. I didn't believe all his threats, but even half of them would be bad enough.

'Can we come to some sort of agreement about this? If I take this job, will you leave me alone? I thought we'd agreed to put all this business behind us.'

'Listen to me, Gornostayev. I inherited you from Belov, and there were no conditions in the will, no restrictions and no agreements. You're in my pocket now. The most you can do is try and bite my finger. Now off you go, and wait nicely for the postman.'

I stepped out onto the pavement. The car's window hummed as it wound down. 'I might call you. And as for you, Viktor Nikolayevich, you can call me "Arkady".'

'The name's Kärppä,' I stammered to the closing window, and even I could hear the hollowness in my voice.

I received the package from Arkady the following day. The microfilms arrived in an envelope purporting to be a statement from American Express. I must have underestimated Arkady's professionalism at our first meeting. Along with the rolls of film was a sheet of paper listing which films belonged to which church records. The note was written in Finnish, and it was signed simply 'A'. Then: 'P.S. I've been keeping an eye on your hard work. I've asked around. Nobody has seen the Tallinn girl. Careful what you get yourself mixed up in.'

What was I supposed to think about this? I agonized; at the very least, I was well and truly in the shit, and the thought of my every last move being watched didn't make me feel any better about it. I paced up and down the office floor, sitting every now and then, rocking back and forth in the office chair. I played Tetris, gnawed the end of my pen and racked my brain.

I knew I'd have to try and keep on top of things, try to climb out of this mess by myself. Karpov wouldn't be any use, and Ryshkov was doubtless involved in too many dirty dealings with the Federal Security Service or other former KGB organizations to be of any help. Arkady seemed to know a lot about my business, but surely the Russian embassy didn't have enough staff these days to keep track of small fry like me, I tried to reason with myself. Someone in my close circle must have informed on me. That someone might very well have been Ryshkov.

Could Korhonen help me out? No. There was no way I could go to him and say, 'Listen, I've got a bit of a problem. There's a Russian spy asking me to do some business for him, picking up where the last Russian spy left off.' He would have asked how much the Russian embassy had profited from my loyal custom; then he'd turn me over to the intelligence services, and I could wave farewell to Finland for good.

I put the microfilms in a plastic envelope, wrenched the filing cabinet from the wall and taped the envelope to the back of the cabinet. The trip to Mikkeli would have to wait; now I had to concentrate on Sirje Larsson, at least for a while. Perhaps that would allow my subconscious to tick along and come up with a way to get rid of Arkady.

I booked tickets for the catamaran crossing the following morning, called Ryshkov's men in Tallinn and sorted myself out with a car. I planned to talk to Sirje's friends from the art course, and was thinking about how to find the community college in the phone book. My concise encyclopaedia saved me: it pointed me in the direction of the adult-education centre, which was listed under the city's municipal services. Before long I was walking up the steps to the Keskinen Art College in the Kallio neighbourhood.

Sirje's teacher, a visual artist who looked like a civil servant, listened to me with a friendly demeanour, but all he could remember about Sirje Larsson was that she was a 'bold exponent of the colour yellow'. He had no knowledge of her life outside the classroom. The other students were working diligently on their canvases in unsettling silence. They were women, middle-aged or slightly older, and at the far end of the room was a solitary retired gentleman who was painting something small and intricate and who seemed utterly focused on his brush and tubes of paint.

I waited until the lesson was over and wandered round the classroom, asking about Sirje. The ladies smiled pleasantly, but explained that they simply took part in the course; other than that, the students didn't have anything to do with one another. They glanced up at each other, then returned to their work, fully absorbed. Once the class came to an end, they said their goodbyes and quickly filed out of the classroom like a group of over-excitable teenagers at break time. In the corridor, one of the women slowed, hesitated for a moment and then turned to me. I walked over to her.

'Esko and Sirje were... friends, you might say. They chatted a lot, at the beginning and end of the class, and they often left together. Sirje lives in Pakila, doesn't she? She took the bus home; they might have walked to the bus stop together, I don't know,' she said, her voice lowered, seemingly content with her covert information.

'Esko. You mean the old boy at the back of the class?' I asked.

'No, that's Unto. Esko Turunen is much younger,' she corrected me, then stressed: 'I doubt there was anything untoward going on.'

I imagined she was looking forward to the following week's class, when she would be able to confide in the other students. There was more to Sirje and Esko's friendship than just oil painting, she'd say; that's what that man was asking about...

'Esko Turunen?' I repeated, to double check. 'You wouldn't happen to know where this Turunen lives?'

At first the woman shook her head, then hastily dug a notebook from her bag, took out a sheet of folder paper and handed it to me. It was a photocopy of contact details for everyone on the course. I recognized Sirje Larsson's tiny, even handwriting. She had written down her home address and given numbers for both the landline and her private mobile. The name 'Esko Turunen' was written in a left-slanting hand. I tried to remember whether this was considered an attempt at originality or a sign of mental illness. His address was given simply as 'Lapinlahdenkatu'; I saved the telephone number in my mobile.

I thanked the helpful woman, half ran back to Hakaniemi and fetched my car from the courtyard. My parking space was tight; a van belonging to one of the local fishmongers was parked right up against my Volvo, and I had to first shove the rubbish bins out of the way then clamber into the car via the passenger seat.

Directory enquiries recognized Esko Turunen's phone number and provided me with an address: Lapinlahdenkatu 12. I drove along Kaisaniemenkatu and headed downtown, past the railway and bus stations towards Kamppi, swerved onto Lapinlahdenkatu and located number 12 close to the Maria General Hospital. I remembered the hospital's old building. I had once driven an elderly Ingrian man up here and interpreted for him. On the door was an antique sign in Finnish and Russian: FIRST AID AND BANDAGING FOR AILING AND WOUNDED SOLDIERS. The old man had been entranced by it.

I rang the downstairs doorbell. The name TURUNEN E. had been typed out on a red plastic ribbon. The electric lock on the door remained closed. I peered up at the windows, but couldn't work out which ones belonged to which apartments. I fetched my satchel from the boot of the car and loitered on the street for about ten minutes until the door opened and a girl appeared, her hair jutting to the side and tied up with elastic bands that looked to me like doughnuts. I nattered to her about how lucky it was she'd opened the door, as I had to go and see a friend living upstairs. The girl muttered something blunt and rich in consonants, from which I concluded she couldn't care less about unfamiliar men wandering around in the stairwell.

Turunen lived on the third floor, his windows facing into the courtyard. The stairwell was tidy, dry and warm. From my satchel I took out a stethoscope and pressed it against the surface of the door. I could hear music coming from inside the apartment; the Latin melody and female voice sounded familiar, though I couldn't put a name to them. I kept my eyes firmly fixed on the stairwell, but was able to listen in peace, as there was nobody there to disapprove of my little game of doctors and nurses. A few times I heard bangs coming from inside the apartment, the sounds of movement or of moving furniture. Esko Turunen was home.

I put the stethoscope back in my satchel and gave the doorbell a businesslike ring. I waited, then rang again. The door remained firmly closed. Again I took out my doctor's equipment; now the apartment was as quiet as an old woman's slipper. I rattled the doorbell and knocked at the door, but Turunen was in no mind to answer.

I stopped to think. This art-school classmate was the only slender lead I had to sniff around. My reward was waiting to be claimed, but from the faint noises inside the apartment it was hard to say whether or not Sirje Larsson was in there. I called for the elevator – it was an old model

– and opened the grille as loudly as possible. I took the lift down to the ground floor, rattled the outer door, then slipped back inside, snuck through the stairwell and out into the courtyard.

The building was old and the apartments didn't have individual balconies. Turunen's windows were dark, but I almost laughed out loud when, a few minutes later, a light was switched on inside. 'I'll meet you yet, Turunen, trust me,' I promised, to myself more than anything.

9

I had only spoken to my contact in Tallinn by phone. He had given me the bare minimum of information – black leather jacket and a grey Toyota Camry – and assumed we'd find each other.

Boris Kovalyov was right. He might as well have been carrying a sign saying: RUSSIAN CROOK. He was a beefy chap, shorter than me, and his knee-length leather jacket sagged round his shoulders. Kovalyov was leaning against his car's front fender, smoking a cigarette and wearing no hat or gloves, though a cold wind was blowing through the harbour. He shook my hand and flicked his cigarette end onto the asphalt. I sat in the front seat of the Toyota and saw that there was another fellow slouched in the back seat.

'Kolya works for us; he's a bit tired. We'll drop him home on the way,' said Kovalyov, and started driving. I looked round at the passenger in the back. Kolya seemed to be out for the count. Kovalyov steered the car with one hand, while with the other he reached into the glove compartment, took out a pistol and gave it to me. The car was plain and shabby, though it wasn't particularly old. It smelled of tobacco and Wunderbaum air freshener. The shock absorbers clanked into action as we drove across a manhole, and every time we braked it felt as though the car was swerving and juddering to the left.

Again I looked over my shoulder. I could see Kolya's eyelids twitching and noticed that there were no cars behind us. With my left hand I yanked up the handbrake, and with my right I pulled the keys from the ignition. The Toyota glided a short distance forward then came to a stop in the middle of the road.

'This isn't good, you know. In fact, this is really bad.' My voice tightened, and I took hold of Kovalyov's face with the palm of my hand. His lips pursed like a child offering a kiss. I turned his head round to face me and leaned closer. 'This is completely fucked up. I asked you to sort me out with a smart car, not a limousine – just something that will take me through the city for 20 kilometres. I told you in plain Russian that I was only coming to see a few people, then heading back to Helsinki.'

I squeezed Kovalyov's cheeks a bit harder. The man said nothing; he didn't struggle or fight back.

'And what do I get? A third-grade crook who hands me a gun in the car park in broad daylight, the car might as well be a tractor from Turkmenistan and comes complete with a young athlete in the back seat who's overdosed on steroids. Not quite what I had in mind.'

I let go of his face. Kovalyov rubbed his cheeks and began to explain, his hands and body following the contours of his words.

'We know, we understand… Ryshkov just told us to help Vitya, Vitya is a good guy. And I thought, it's always good to have a gun. It's legit, too,' Kovalyov assured me. 'Kolya was fine this morning. I don't know when he managed to shoot up. He's not at his best right now, I'll say that much, and this car is, well...'

'Boris, I don't give flying fuck about his body clock or the paperwork for the motor,' I said. 'I'm going for a walk. Fifteen minutes. Do whatever the hell you've got to do to get rid of this banger and ditch our map-reader, find me a smarter car and meet me back here. You've got fifteen minutes, and half of it's already gone. Now move it.'

I slammed the door shut. Kovalyov revved the motor and sped away. The Camry left behind a cloud of bluish exhaust fumes and the fug of burnt oil.

I realized I didn't know much about Ryshkov's business matters in Tallinn. I knew he transported bootlegged CDs from Estonia to Finland, but these two looked like they were in the drug trade – as customers, at the very least. The more I thought about the different aspects of Ryshkov's dodgy dealings, the more unnerved I became.

In the end I waited for about twenty minutes before Kovalyov returned, this time in a Volkswagen Transporter.

'Not in a truck this time, eh?' I was tough with my contact, but didn't reprimand him for being late.

It seemed Kolya had either been left asleep in the Toyota or moved somewhere else. The minivan was relatively neat, though the air freshener smelled like a toilet duck. Sitting in the middle seat of the Volkswagen, hands resting on the back of the seat in front of him was a Central Asian-looking guy, who turned his head and eyed me up and down as though he couldn't care less what kind of client he had to escort around the city.

'Karim is one of our boys, too,' Kovalyov informed me. 'Arrived last week from Dushanbe.' I nodded at Karim. He blinked his eyes.

'All I needed was a lift,' I told Kovalyov.

'"Proper help for Viktor," that's what Ryshkov said. Well, the Toyota was a bit of a cock-up and Kolya wasn't in good shape. But it'll be fine. Trust me.' We set off.

The light-coloured apartment block in the Lillemäe suburb of Tallinn was tidy, but about as memorable as the seven identical buildings standing next to it. Kovalyov parked the Volkswagen by the side of the street and glanced restlessly in the mirrors. He would have been more at home in the dark alleyways around Kopli or Mustamäe than here in an area populated mostly by Estonians.

I told him to stay in the car and listen to an Estonian station on the radio. To Karim, I said nothing. I clapped the door shut and prepared myself to meet the parents of Sirje and Jaak Lillepuu.

'Are you a descendent of defected Communists, or what?' Paul Lillepuu boomed before I'd had the chance to put a full stop after my introductory sentence. He was a short, sturdy man whose age was hard to gauge. Sirje's mother remained seated calmly in an armchair as her husband stood up to his full five-foot-four stature. An image of my own mother and father flashed through my mind: what kind of elderly married couple would they be now, if my father were still alive?

'Ingrian on my father's side; my mother came from Finland with her parents when she was a girl,' I explained. To reassure him, I added: 'They were Communists.'

'That's all behind us now, but I don't have much time for Communists.' Paul Lillepuu spoke good Finnish. Aino Lillepuu remained silent. From the few words she'd spoken,

I realized that she, too, understood Finnish fully, though she was shy to speak it.

'Aarne is paying you to look for Sirje. Good job. Our boy is a bad apple. I telephoned him and told him his sister is missing, and all he said was: "I'm not interested." I said my farewells years ago. That hooligan can go to hell.' Paul Lillepuu's voice trembled with agitation. Aino Lillepuu dabbed the corners of her eyes.

I tried to ask the elderly couple questions that would allow them to retain their dignity. They showed me Sirje's belongings from her time in Tallinn. A couple of shoeboxes contained the prized possessions of a young schoolgirl during the Soviet era: cassettes of music by Western rock groups, diaries from fifteen years ago, out-of-focus photographs of young people trying to dress fashionably.

Memories of Sortavala pushed their way into my mind. Treasures from my own past, gifts I'd received from Finnish tourists: a plastic bag with the words CARLSSON DEPARTMENT STORE KUOPIO printed on it, ballpoint pens with logos and a ski hat emblazoned with an image of a squirrel and the name of a Finnish bank. My mother's annoyance at beggars, illegitimate business and having to change money.

I must call my mother, I reminded myself.

I forced my mind back to Tallinn. Aino Lillepuu gently gripped Sirje's photograph in her fingers. She spoke Finnish slowly and deliberately, searching for words, repeating herself.

'We don't understand what has happened. Sirje is a good girl; she enjoyed being with Aarne. And Aarne is a good man, even though he's older than her and can sometimes be a… *harsh* man. I don't believe Sirje has taken off on an adventure. And Jaak assured us Sirje has nothing to do with his business affairs, so nobody has any reason to harm her. We are very grateful you've come to help us.'

I fetched a pint of beer and a slice of pizza from the bar. The journey to Helsinki took only an hour and a half on the large catamaran, enough time for a few slow pints. I'd just opened a detective novel I'd packed for the trip when a man's hand pressed the book against the table. 'Let's go for a smoke,' a voice said above my head. The hand moved and closed around my wrist. The grip was firm, and the hand large. Veins stood out along the man's arm like pipes. I didn't bother claiming not to smoke, and duly stood up. We walked towards the deck at the back of the catamaran.

A cold wind whipped across the small deck reserved for smokers. Waiting for us were two thickset men in their thirties, one wearing a grey jacket and the other a suede coat. Neither complained about the chill.

I was about to assure them I was ready to cooperate when the man in the suede jacket gripped my shoulder and yanked my arm painfully behind my back. The man who'd fetched me came to his assistance, and together they hauled me unnecessarily far over the railings; the banister around the smoking area pressed into my thighs just above the knee. I looked straight down into the churning blue-grey waters. The sea mist sprayed up into my face, and I focused on my fears.

'You're visiting the wrong places, asking the wrong questions, messing with the wrong business,' I heard the steady voice above the roar of the engines. From the accent, I could tell that the speaker was Estonian, though he expressed himself in Finnish without giving it a second thought.

'The girl has disappeared. So what? It's a family matter, Aarne Larsson's family matter. I've got nothing to do with it, and neither have my mother and father. Now let them grieve in peace.' The man intensified the force of his words by shoving a hard object against my anus. With my head dangling downwards and a pistol in my backside, I couldn't speak.

'Have you understood everything I've said?' Jaak Lillepuu growled with a painful thrust of his pistol. 'If not, I'll make sure you never have trouble with haemorrhoids again. I dread to think where the bullet might end up. You get my drift?'

I whimpered and nodded my head. I tried to imagine the trajectory of that bullet and felt my testicles draw up towards my body; my prostate gland gave a twinge, and my stomach muscles started to cramp. The men wrenched me back onto the deck; my mobile phone came clattering out of my pocket, and one of the bruisers hurled it into the Baltic Sea. I didn't put up a fight. *Nokia – Connecting Fish,* I thought to myself, but didn't share the joke with my new acquaintances.

Jaak Lillepuu replaced his pistol in his pocket and looked me squarely in the eye. 'Don't disturb elderly folk,' he said pointedly. He was a handsome man, more like his mother than his father. There might even have been a family resemblance to Sirje.

He slowly lit up, crumpled his empty cigarette packet, slam-dunked it into the rubbish bin and smoked in deep, slow drags. Lillepuu's henchmen loosened their grip on my arms and stood silently to one side.

We all watched as Lillepuu smoked. He flicked his cigarette end over the railings and turned towards me. 'Do I make myself clear,' he said, more a statement than a question, and stepped inside. The two bodyguards followed behind him. I remained on the smoking deck alone.

My heart was still beating erratically with fear, but I dashed to the rubbish bin and dug out the Marlboro packet Lillepuu had thrown into the trash. I hadn't been mistaken: SELECTED FINE TOBACOS. The spelling mistake was there, on the side of the packet.

10

The forecourt outside Ruuskanen's Quality Motors on the ring road was bumpy, covered in slush and cordoned off with mesh fencing. The Volvo juddered into it, and I pulled up to the shack that served as an office. About fifty cars were parked outside. The most attractive Mercedes and BMWs had been positioned right by the ring road, and behind them, slightly hidden, was a row of Renaults, Nissans and Toyotas, their paintwork faded and pocked with rust.

Ruuskanen appeared to be assessing the value of a red Opel Kadett. A young man with spiky hair had shown interest in a sporty-looking black Mazda, and Ruuskanen was prowling round the Opel the client wanted to trade in, looking it up and down, assessing the paintwork, the interior and the condition of the tires. He spoke in an encouraging, fatherly tone. I'd seen this particular piece of theatre before, and I knew that Ruuskanen was praising the Kadett's condition and thinking of a trade price out loud, as though he didn't know what he was doing. 'It's in surprisingly good nick for a car this old. We'll have to pay you something for this one.'

I was about to laugh out loud when Ruuskanen's business partner Taivassalo walked out of the office, fidgeting with a set of keys and pretending to be on his way somewhere else before stopping next to the Opel. He dropped to his knees and felt around the chassis before opening the boot and pulling up the mat on the floor of the vehicle. Taivassalo muttered away to himself: 'Dear oh dear, rust, rust, rust.' He sat in the driver's seat, turned on the ignition and revved the motor so that black fumes billowed from the exhaust pipe. Using only first gear and reverse, he forced the car a metre forwards and back again, then switched off the motor.

I stepped closer and heard Taivassalo give Ruuskanen his carefully considered opinion.

'The engine will need to be completely overhauled; the clutch is slipping and the gearbox is playing up, too. The chassis is riddled with rust – the bodywork is a wreck, and there are dents in the hubcaps.'

Ruuskanen continued as though in the same breath as his partner: 'So, if you throw in a set of summer tires, I'll give you six thousand for it.'

The young man could do nothing but accept the offer and glumly shook on it, though from reading the ads in car magazines and the Yellow Pages, he'd been sure he'd get at least 15,000 marks for his old Kadett.

I followed the deal brokers into the office shack, sat down on the battered customer bench and flicked through dog-eared copies of old car magazines. Ruuskanen took out the car's registration papers, asked for the young man's details and promised he would sort out the paperwork. The customer left to fetch the remaining money and a set of summer tires.

'So what do you think of that, Kärppä?' Ruuskanen smiled, chuffed with himself. He was in his fifties, well dressed and a bit on the chubby side. He had a thick head of curls that looked as though a wig had been placed on his round head.

'What's your price for the Kadett?' I asked straight out.

'Seventeen to eighteen K at least, but I'll sell it for about twelve. We'll have to tweak a few things, then I'll get the documentation: family's second car, not many miles on the clock, straight from the wife's hands. It smells of cigarettes a bit, but women smoke too these days, eh?'

I told him to spare me the sales pitch and asked him to lend me a relatively tidy, nondescript car for a day. Ruuskanen didn't ask any questions, but took a set of keys out of the drawer and threw them at me. 'What's mine is yours. The red Mondeo. Don't smash it up.'

The Quality Motors label dangling from the Ford's mirror read: 'Fully MOT Certified!' I trusted the car would survive the 30 kilometres I needed it for – and more importantly, I knew that Aarne Larsson wouldn't recognize it.

I drove to Stenbäckinkatu, parked a few cars' distance from Larsson's bookshop and began my stakeout. Radio Suomi was playing a selection of old dancehall classics. I learned plenty as I sat there listening: Dallapé was an orchestra that had been going for decades; Vili Vesterinen was an accordion virtuoso; and Jori Malmsten composed lots of songs. Many of the melodies were familiar. I used to listen to Finnish radio broadcasts back home in Karelia. In Leningrad, my flatmates had generally preferred European rock stations that felt more dangerous or prohibited, but in Sortavala we listened to the National Radio.

Only a few customers visited Larsson's shop, and it seemed they really were all buying books. Perhaps the shop made a profit after all, I mused, though my thoughts were still preoccupied with the events of my trip to Tallinn. Why did Jaak Lillepuu have cigarettes from Karpov's missing shipment, and why had Jaak spoken of his sister as though she were dead? *Let our parents grieve in peace*. That's what he'd told me to do, while suggesting that Sirje's disappearance was a matter for the Larsson couple alone.

Ryshkov had given me a new mobile, and I copied phone numbers from my diary into the phone's memory. Still, an unfortunate number of contact details had sunk to the bottom of the Baltic Sea. It suddenly occurred to me that Sirje, too, must have had a mobile phone. Where was it now? There was no phone book in the Larssons' house, only a few entries in the calendar on the table. The numbers saved in that phone's memory might help reveal something. I locked the Ford and stepped into Larsson's shop.

'Sirje does have a mobile phone, and it's with her now. Of course, I've tried to contact her on that number regularly, and left messages on her voicemail,' Larsson explained as though I were a child.

He was standing behind the counter in a cardigan with patches of blue suede on the elbows. I was annoyed at myself for not asking about the phone sooner.

'It seems to me, Kärppä, as though you expect this case to solve itself. Either that or you think I'm somehow impeding you. I really thought you were up to the job,' said Larsson, working himself up and twisting the frames of his reading glasses. 'I thought you had some Finnish guts about you, but you're as pathetic as any Russian. They've ruined you.'

Larsson's voice tightened further. 'Damn it, man, I expect you to find out where Sirje is or tell me what's happened to her. And I want to know, no matter how unpleasant the truth might be.'

I assured him as calmly as possible that I would do everything I could to solve the case. I walked back to the car and took a deep breath once I'd sat down in the front seat and locked the door. Larsson and his bookshop sent a chill across my skin.

Igor Pervukhin's telephone number had disappeared into the sea, but directory enquiries found a contact number for my old friend from St Petersburg. Igor had landed himself a job in telecommunications, a job that I didn't understand much about except that it appeared Igor was some kind of genius. From our time in Leningrad, all I remembered was his talent as a DJ at the local youth club. He used to play Western rock music, precious vinyls that were hard to come by; he would mumble his incomprehensible introductions into a microphone, shake his limp, black hair up and down and brag about the gradient tint in his spectacles. I'd last seen him back in the autumn, and it seemed he had remained true to the style of his youth.

Igor assured me he was still working for the same telecommunications firm. 'You know, online programming, that kind of stuff…' he began. I cut him off while I still understood what he was talking about.

'Listen, my friend, can you help me? I'm interested in the mobile phone details for one Sirje Larsson. The phone will either be registered to that name, or to Aarne Larsson, or Larsson's Collectible Books,' I explained in Russian. I repeated the names again just to be sure and gave him the Larssons' various addresses. Pervukhin told me not to get my hopes up, but promised he'd see what he could find and get back to me.

11

Ryshkov turned up at the office and asked me to follow him: 'A small job. I need an assistant.'

I tried to ask what it was about, but Ryshkov chivvied me out of the door.

'Gennady, you know I don't want to get involved in any drug deals. Your boys in Tallinn were a pretty screwed-up bunch,' I dared to complain.

'It's nothing like that.' He shook his head as he stepped into his Mercedes. I locked up the office and hopped into the passenger seat. The car was tidy and warm, and a golden cross dangled from the mirror.

'So, can you still judge the engine power just by putting your foot on the pedal?' I asked as Ryshkov sped away from the traffic lights, but he said nothing.

We drove to the Lahti highway. Ryshkov took the Pihlajamäki exit and drove past Malmi Cemetery, turned onto the road running alongside the railway tracks and continued past the airport towards the area of Puistola.

'Where are we going?' I couldn't help enquiring.

'We're going to pay a visit to a guy who owes me,' Ryshkov explained. 'You can do the talking. He's Finnish.' He turned onto a smaller road. The streets seemed to be organized in a grid, and the entire area was as even and unsurprising as the open hectares of land around the airport, which could just be made out behind the row of alders at the side of the road. The houses, however, seemed randomly positioned on their respective plots, and brand new, fully renovated properties stood side-by-side with wonky, dilapidated old cottages.

'He lives over there.' Ryshkov nodded towards a wooden, yellow house. He drove some way past it, then brought the car to a halt. We got out. Ryshkov locked the doors with his remote-control key, and the lights flickered as the car registered the command.

We walked into the yard. The owner hadn't cleared the snow all winter. Repeated footsteps had beaten a path from the street to the front door; day after day it had melted and refrozen to form a slippery trench.

Ryshkov stepped inside first. The front door only half-opened before catching on the layer of ice covering the porch. I followed him from the dim hallway into the kitchen. The cottage stank of stale tobacco smoke and the dampness of an old building.

A woman was sitting at the kitchen table, a black cardigan round her shoulders, smoking a cigarette that looked like she'd rolled it herself and flicking ash into a glass jar. Yellowed cigarette ends floated in the tar-brown liquid that reached to the upper edge of the jar's torn label. I could just make out what was left of the text: PICKLED CUCUMB.

'Where's Timo?' Ryshkov asked slowly in Finnish.

'Just left. Must have seen you coming,' the woman replied, and turned towards us. Her face was gaunt, pale and jaundiced. A row of rings dangled from her ear, and she had a stud through her nose. Her black hair fell across her shoulders.

'I've nothing to do with his business,' she added, and then nodded towards the bedroom: 'He went that way.' I went to take a look: the window was swinging open, and in the crumpled sheets I could make out the impressions left by Timo's shoes as he'd jumped out. In a photograph on the wall, somebody's grandparents stared accusingly at the activities of their descendants.

I clambered onto the window ledge and jumped. It was only a one-metre drop into the soft snow below. A red Christmas decoration caught my sleeve – a clumsy image of a dancing elf glued onto a piece of red card. I didn't know whether it had been left there from last Christmas or forgotten since the 1980s, but I tried to prise it from my clothes intact and chucked the red old man back through the window.

I was able to hop across the footprints Timo had left behind. He'd waded through the snow towards the perimeter fence around the airport. At the end of the garden was a narrow vegetable patch, now overgrown with bushes, and after that a jogging track running the length of the fence. A skier in a brightly coloured outfit sped past. I looked first to the left, then to the right, and again to the left. About a hundred metres away I saw a man running in the wrong direction to be out for an evening jog.

I dashed along the ski trail and shouted at him to stop. He didn't pay any notice, but tried to speed up instead. I caught up with him and shoved him with the full force of my body in the way only a Premier League footballer knows how. The man staggered into the snow-covered verge. I waited. He got up, dusted the snow from his face and stood gasping for breath. I stepped closer to him and took hold of his green bomber jacket in case he tried anything. Timo was taller then me, but I could tell from his eyes that at that moment he felt particularly small.

A helicopter flew low above us and prepared to land on the field. It had appeared out of nowhere. I felt the sound of the rotor blades in my stomach. My mind was suddenly flooded with images from my time in the army, like a film reel, complete with colours and sounds. I recalled how we'd practised disembarking from a helicopter in the middle of a swamp in full kit, and how my cabin mate Sushlov had wept with exhaustion. He was afraid of Afghanistan, worried he wouldn't cut it in training or in our regiment.

I remembered how Sushlov had gripped my arm and asked me to help him, to understand him, and how I'd quietly told him I couldn't help him, didn't have the energy. A while later, Yevgeny Sushlov was dismissed and sent home, apparently for psychological problems. Rumour had it he'd been caught having a homosexual encounter in the barracks. He should think himself lucky he didn't end up in prison or a psychiatric ward.

All this I remembered in a flash. The helicopter whipped up the snow on the runway, far away on the other side of the field. Ryshkov had caught up with me, stepping gingerly through the snow in his brogues. Eventually, he stepped into a snowdrift, hauled the man back onto the running track and dragged him a short distance to the patch where, in the summer months, joggers on the track would stand doing abdominal and back exercises on a set of trestles and work out with wooden weights.

Ryshkov shoved the man against the weights stand. 'Tell the little shit he's got a week to cough up the money he owes me,' Ryshkov hissed in Russian, his eyes boring into the Finn's.

'He says you're a little shit, and you've got a week to pay what you owe him,' I repeated evenly, like an interpreter at a conference. Timo nodded and mumbled quietly. I couldn't make out the words.

With one arm, Ryshkov lifted one of the weight logs into the air; with his other arm, he held Timo's hand on a piece of rubber tire nailed in place to soften the thud of the falling weights. Next to the rubber surface was the side of a tire. All that remained of the manufacturer's logo were the letters UN.

Dunlop, I thought. *Or Uniroyal.* I almost shouted out loud when Ryshkov dropped the weight on Timo's hand.

'Ow,' he said. He didn't yell, didn't scream, simply lifted his feet one after the other like a dog with frozen paws.

'Christ, you didn't give him much warning. I'll bet that hurt,' I said, shuddering, trying to lighten the mood, but Ryshkov didn't get it and Timo didn't find it funny. Ryshkov walked off towards the cottage. I was about to follow him, but turned back and lifted the wooden weight. Timo was holding his hand, carefully trying to move his fingers, and eventually stuck his entire hand up to the wrist in the snow. I hurried after Ryshkov.

We retraced our footprints. This time we didn't go in through the window but walked round the side of the cottage, steadied ourselves on snow hardened by water dripping from the gutter, reached the path to the yard and found the road and the car. Ryshkov drove off, pulled a Marlboro out of his pocket and lit up. I could see his hands were steady, but his brow and black hair were sweaty.

'I like you, Vitya,' he said, as though starting a presentation. 'But you work for me. And I like lots of guys who work for me. Boris in Tallinn is one of them. And it upset me when I heard how you behaved when you were there.' Ryshkov emphasized every word. 'In fact, it really pissed me off. You are like a glove, a wrench, at most a drill. And in my tool kit there are only reliable tools.'

I nodded to show I had understood.

12

The sight of Timo's mangled fingers flashed through my mind as I tried to fish a pickled gherkin from the barrel at the store in Hakaniemi. My mobile phone rang, and I had to hold the plastic bag under my arm as I tried to answer it.

It was Karpov from Sortavala.

'Viktor, I want you to sit down and not to panic,' he said. My knees went limp. 'Your mother's in hospital. She's in a pretty bad way, but she's in good hands now, and I'm sure she'll make a full recovery.'

Karpov told me my mother had had a heart attack that morning. A neighbour had spotted her slumped on the porch with an empty shopping bag beneath her arm, and taken her to the hospital. Karpov had found out about it and arranged for the other patients in the room to be moved elsewhere, paid the doctors a little extra and made sure the hospital was stocked with good medication.

He ended the call. Somehow I had managed to thank him, and stood there leaning against the meat counter. I'd gone through this scenario in my mind when I'd first moved to Finland, and my mother wanted to stay in Sortavala. But the real situation was different; it was a punch in the gut as though from a heavyweight boxer, and after the initial shock it left you with a strange mixture of panic and paralysis.

I paid for my groceries, went home and tried to make some dinner, but my thoughts kept running back to Sortavala. I could see the hospital room, nurses creeping along the endless corridors, my mother in a small hospital bed. I tortured myself by imagining her funeral. Pain rushed through my chest when I thought of the arrival of spring in Sortavala, the trees tentatively coming into leaf, the first eager coltsfoots, all the things Mother might not live to see.

All I could do was worry about things from a distance. I called the hospital. A supervisor told me in an officious monotone that my mother's situation was stable, that she was very tired and was now asleep. More than that, he either couldn't or wouldn't tell me, and the registrar was currently in theatre.

Then I called Karpov, apologized for bugging him every five minutes and told him I was coming to Sortavala. I'd be there the following morning. He promised to look after me and assured me someone would be on guard at the hospital, round the clock. I thought of Karpov's men, all skinheads in leather jackets with no distinguishing features other than the details of their tattoos. Mother would hardly need chocolate and tangerines, I said, so the boys can stay in the corridor. Karpov could go in and tell her I was on my way. 'Tell her that. Say it out loud, even if she's asleep.'

Karpov promised he would, and reminded me that my mother had fed him many times over the years and let him spend many nights under her roof. He would take care of everything. I even remembered to ask him to get hold of two Soviet-Army-style rubber dinghies and fur hats. A trader at the market had asked me to bring some back for him, and I didn't have the time or inclination to drive all the way to Vyborg to get them. Besides, there was such demand for rubber dinghies at the moment that there were none left at the barracks of the Karelian regiments. You had to import them from further afield in Russia. Karpov calmly assured me he would arrange for the goods to be delivered. In practice, that meant they were already on their way.

I sat for a moment, thought hard and tried to calm down. I decided to clear my desk, find a car suitable for a long journey, get a few hours' sleep and drive through the night. First off, I called my brother Alexei in Moscow. The line crackled with metallic sounds echoing and disappearing into space. Then came Alexei's voice, as clear as if I'd been calling someone a few miles away. I explained the situation briefly, speaking Finnish deliberately, though Alexei had to fumble for words.

My brother had lived in Moscow for about twenty years. He had a career in a privatized oil company, a desk carved from walnut, a lazy secretary and a corrupt boss, a wife at home, a son I hardly knew who was almost an adult, and an extended family on his wife's side living around the towns of Kolomna and Ryazan along the Moscow River. We weren't on bad terms; it's just that we didn't have much to do with each other. But he was still my mother's son. Alexei was shocked, and promised to get to Sortavala as quickly as possible.

I packed a couple of bags of clothes, ate what was left in the fridge and made sure the apartment was in a fit state to be left for a few days. Then I returned to the office and read my email. I sent Ryshkov a message bringing him up to speed about my mother and the forthcoming trip. I called Larsson. He didn't pick up, but I left a message on the answering machine saying I was on a short trip to Sortavala, but that I would continue my search for Sirje while I was away.

Ruuskanen agreed to lend me a Mercedes registered to his company and some legal paperwork so I didn't have to explain myself at the border. The Mondeo was still waiting in the street. They could take it back to the dealer.

For a moment I hesitated, then pulled up the homepage of the University of Helsinki and a list of contact email addresses. I wrote:

Hello, Marja – I hope you are the right Marja Takala. In brief, I've been thinking about you a lot. It would be nice to see you or talk on the phone, perhaps. I hope you don't find this message intrusive. I will be away for a few days, but let's be in touch.

Best regards,

Kärppä

I changed the closing to *Warm regards* and quickly sent the message before I could change my mind.

I was surprisingly calm as I drove north along Highway 6. Kouvola, Lappeenranta, Imatra. The towns' sleepy junctions appeared out of nowhere and vanished just as quickly. The road was empty and peaceful, but for the glaring headlights of oncoming trucks, which emitted blinding light in all directions. I was calm because I knew I was heading for Sortavala. Before I arrived, there was nothing I could do; I couldn't worry or fret and affect my mother's condition in any way.

Sirje Larsson, the threats made by Jaak Lillepuu, Arkady's microfilms, Ryshkov's dodgy business affairs and the thought of Timo's fingers beneath the wooden weight seemed like distant memories. I simply drove and listened to the radio in the Mercedes, which was, apparently, a decommissioned taxi.

I'd managed to drive in peace and quiet as far as Tohmajärvi, and even had breakfast and got into line on the Finnish side of the border crossing at Värtsilä before my phone finally rang.

'I got your message,' Gennady Ryshkov began calmly. 'Take as long as you need. I'll take care of things in Helsinki. Ask around about the tobacco shipment stolen from Karpov. Tell Valery I think the Estonians are behind it. One of Lillepuu's men is bragging around the city about how he made Stroganoff out of a couple of stuffed Russian suits.'

Ryshkov said he'd take extra supplies to the bootleggers at the Porvoo rest area, and that he thought he'd get by on his day-to-day business for a few weeks. He gave his best regards to my mother, and ended the call. I was taken aback. Ryshkov had spoken gently, at considerable length and hadn't said a word about the little *tête-à-tête* we'd had earlier. I tried to get my head round it and stared at the even, grey morning sky. The cars in front edged forward, and a space the length of a few cars opened up in the queue. The sound of someone beeping their horn snapped me back to reality.

I wrenched the Mercedes door open and marched up to the horn-blower, a young man in a suit and tie who shut the locks on the doors of his Nissan when I approached. I rapped on the window. He rolled it down a few centimetres. I spoke to him first in Russian, then continued in broken Finnish: 'You got a problem?' The man nervously explained that he'd pressed the horn by accident. I got back into my car and drove to the checkpoint.

13

The Finnish customs officers didn't care much for those travelling to Russia. On the Russian side of the checkpoint was the usual group of serious, sleepy-looking young conscripts wandering around with machine guns, customs officials in blue, border guards in green and secretarial staff in garish make-up. They made sure that every now and then the queue looked long enough; then they retreated to their staffrooms and returned to give smudged stamps on customs documents and other paperwork that would never find its way into any official archive.

I kept my mouth firmly shut, decided not to try to sound friendly or worried and cleared the border formalities in only twenty minutes. I even managed to keep my smirk under control, though I was amused by the memory of something Karpov had said years ago: *You know you're in trouble when a border guard slips on a rubber glove and asks you to follow him.*

I turned off the road to Sortavala and headed towards the old parish of Ruskeala. I remembered the route and quickly found the house situated on a warm hillside, where the sun had already melted patches into the bright covering of snow. The house had been cobbled together from logs, planks and bricks. Perhaps it would be more accurate to say it was still being built. The roughcast on the walls was still unpainted and had turned grey; the hall roof was covered with tarpaulin; and the yard was scattered with concrete blocks and assorted piles of two-by-four, untreated wood and corrugated roofing.

The house wouldn't have garnered any complaints from the Ruskeala town planning association, if such a thing had existed. It fit perfectly into the general aesthetic of the village, a post-Soviet realism whose defining characteristic was its overall unfinished look.

I knocked and stepped into the scullery. A Russian man in his fifties stood up from the table, shook my hand and offered me some tea. I politely declined, saying I was in a hurry; I wanted to get back on the road as quickly as possible. The man didn't insist. Instead, he pulled a taped-up cardboard box from the cupboard beneath the sink and handed it to me. The living-room door opened and a woman in leather trousers stood in the doorway. I caught a glimpse of a child sitting behind her, watching television. On the desk was a computer, screen-saver patterns flickering across its monitor. The woman turned and shut the door behind her.

I went outside, sat in the Mercedes and opened the cardboard box. It contained a passport with my photograph. My name was 'Igor Semyonov', and my father's name was Sergey. I was a Russian national born in Vologda on 4 February 1963. The box also contained a set of keys, a Makarov pistol, a holster, banknotes totalling well over 100,000 roubles, crumpled receipts and papers with texts and stamps in Russian.

I put my Finnish passport and a few thousand marks into the box, keeping some of the Finnish cash for myself and placing it in my wallet alongside the roubles. Among

Semyonov's paperwork was a visa for entry into Finland. It was convenient that Viktor Kärppä always seemed to be abroad when someone such as Semyonov or Larionov or Kuznetsov arrived in Finland for a visit. This time I wasn't planning a visit to Finland, but Karpov was generally meticulous about such plans.

The leather-clad woman walked out to the yard and handed me a bunch of keys. 'You forgot these,' she said, her expression serious, and added: 'The Ruskeala Hertz office would like to thank you for your custom.' She nodded towards the garage bricked up with cement blocks and returned to the house, skipping in her tennis shoes to avoid the worst of the snow.

I opened the heavy lock outside the garage, reversed the Volkswagen Passat with St Petersburg plates out into the street and parked the Mercedes in its place. I lifted my luggage from one trunk and put it in the other. I pulled on my gloves, picked up the pistol and checked the magazine, not wanting to leave my prints on a gun I knew nothing about. The weapon was very likely documented and catalogued as being currently in a garrison somewhere in central Russia, but it could have been used to kill someone – the bullets, pulled from the victims, now waiting in the militia archives for the gun to turn up.

I placed the Makarov beneath the driver's seat in the Passat, locked the garage and took the cardboard box back to the man sitting in the cottage. I didn't stick around to see where he hid it, but I knew he would look after my things. I started the engine and set off towards Sortavala.

'Mother,' I said quietly in Finnish. My mother was asleep; she looked small and brittle. A drip was taped to her forearm and a tube disappeared up her nose. More wires and cables twisted from beneath her blankets. An array of efficient-looking equipment stood around her. A drip was propped on a stand next to the bed, and various other monitors beeped quietly. A yellow-green strip of light passed the screen, jumping in exactly the same part of the screen in time with her heartbeat. Karpov must have hijacked a cargo of emergency supplies on its way to Moscow to get this kind of gear.

'Mother...' I repeated. She was asleep and breathing evenly, but suddenly opened her eyes. Her grey eyes stared at the ceiling before looking to see where the voice had come from. 'Oh, Viktor,' she smiled, and stretched her fingers towards me. She didn't seem at all surprised to see me. I took her small, soft hand between my two giant fists, gently squeezed it, and smiled.

I stayed with my mother for about half an hour, then left her to rest. She was tired and spoke slowly, occasionally pausing for a long while. I told her I'd be in Sortavala for many days yet, and that I'd come back later that evening. Mother seemed to fall asleep before I'd even reached the door.

Karpov was waiting for me outside the hospital, leaning against the bonnet of his Mercedes. A burly henchman complete with the obligatory sunglasses was standing at the other side of the car.

'Ryshkov called. Said you'd picked up the package. Everything went smoothly?' I nodded. 'Here's the key. The place is heated, and we've stocked up with food, so make yourself at home.'

Karpov threw me the key with a key ring I remembered from our days back in Sortavala.

Our cottage – our home – was situated at the end of a dirt track in Vakkosalmi. It was an old house, originally built by Finns but subsequently mended and renovated in the local Sortavala style. A sense of homecoming caught me as I stepped into the porch, and once inside the cottage it hit me like a warm wave. I took my things into the bedroom.

The table in the scullery was piled with preserves, bread, cake and four bottles of vodka. The fridge was stocked with milk, a length of salami, German sausages, pork chops packaged in Finland, beer, even some oranges and bottled water. I sat down at my own chair beside the familiar table. Only now did I notice I was hungry and thirsty.

That evening, I sat with my mother for an hour. I held her hand and it didn't feel strange, though the last time I'd done so must have been when I was in primary school. She snoozed through most of my visit.

Every now and then, she spoke: 'I'm not in any trouble, but it was tough, mind, and oh, how it hurt… It was as though I could see your father sitting at the end of the bed.'

I listened, replied quietly and felt restless again. Mother's transparent skin was burning with fever. I couldn't remember if I'd ever heard her say something was sore before, or that she didn't have the strength to carry on.

For the most part I stayed at the house and avoided the town. In Karelia there were plenty of men who would have had mischievous thoughts had they'd known I was living by myself in a dilapidated old cottage. I visited my mother by car, and the rest of the time I spent chopping firewood in the shed (which was already stacked full of logs), fixing the television and reading.

Just driving around the town was enough to darken my mind. I watched puffy Finnish men picking up young girls, kids loitering outside restaurants looking for drunken tourists to rob. As I drove I picked out familiar faces, but when I tried to identify them, tried to put names to the figures, I realized I was looking at people of the wrong age. They were young people, whereas anyone I knew would already be middle-aged.

The moonlit evening had chilled and darkened when I heard a car pull up on the street outside. I peered out the scullery window and saw a light-coloured Volga covered in muck. It was standing outside our house, its engine still running and thick smoke belching from the exhaust pipe. My mobile phone rang; I answered without taking my eye off the car outside.

'Hello, Viktor. It's Arkady. How you doing?'

For a few seconds I was speechless. 'Well, I'm... I'm out of town at the moment,' I explained.

'I know,' said Arkady. 'You're in Sortavala. As far as I'm concerned, you're supposed to be in Mikkeli, a place you should have visited long ago. I want to remind you loud and clear that you need to take care of those microfilms. I don't want to have to make this any clearer to you.'

Arkady's tone was formal as his words struck me once again in the gut. 'How's your mother's recovery coming along?'

I gripped the telephone and stared out at the Volga, still billowing smoke into the air. In the darkness, its windows looked black; I couldn't make out anyone inside. Arkady might have been in that car. He could have been in Moscow or Helsinki, but he had arranged for that car to pull up outside the house – of that, there was no doubt.

'Listen, Arkady. I'll take care of your business, but you can be sure I'll take care of you and all your associates if anything happens to my mother. This matter is between you and me. Keep other people out of it.' I tried to speak in a low voice, calmly and carefully.

I heard him hang up at the other end. The Volga continued to wait on the street and belch smoke for a moment longer, then the engine revved up and the car glided forwards.

I went upstairs to the darkened attic and slid my hand into the sawdust and woodchip between the wall panels. The sack was still where I had hidden it years ago. I unwrapped the green cloth and picked up the AK-47 assault rifle. It was standard military issue with a wooden stock. Inside the sack were two magazines and three boxes of cartridges.

The attic was dark, but I closed my eyes, knelt down, took the Kalashnikov apart and put it back together again. My fingers worked almost by themselves. I flicked the selector lever to full automatic, opened the catch lever with my thumb and laid the tin case on the floor, twisted and removed the gas tube and bolt and tipped out the loose carrier spring. I almost jumped to my feet and stood to attention before putting the rifle back together again. In the army we'd practised this drill in daylight, at night, with a sack over our heads, in the fields. Everywhere.

14

'Have you heard anything from Lena?' My mother always knew how to surprise me. I blushed. A grown man.

'Well, no. And I haven't asked after her. The last I heard, Lena was in St Petersburg – but I haven't heard anything for a few years.'

'She is in St Petersburg. She was supposed to be getting together with an engineer, apparently, but something came along and messed things up,' my mother said. 'I know how much the matter with Lena upset you. But you never know, it might never have worked out in the first place. Moving to Finland was hard enough for you, though you speak the language…'

Mother continued filling me in on the local news, and I smiled as I realized she'd regained her strength, though she was still bedridden and relied on the help of others. The monitors and drips had been taken away. Mother had brushed her hair, and her eyes were sharp and alive behind her glasses.

I held her hand. It didn't feel at all strange or awkward.

'I know you'll try and get me to move to Finland with you, but I've lived here all my life and I'll die here, too.' Mother took care of the talking, leaving no room for conversation. 'But not yet, mind. After my first stroke, I thought my time had come. I was so afraid of the pain. I can't bear any more pain.' She explained things calmly, as though it was an everyday matter that had been bothering her. 'But when you walked in here it was like being yanked back to life, and I thought to myself, I'll see this spring and summer yet... I want to.'

We spoke about Alexei's visit. She asked about my work, and I explained in roundabout terms and said I would go back to Finland in the next few days.

'Of course, you can go any time you wish. I'll be right as rain,' she assured me. 'Besides, we've no more business to sort out, no matter how things turn out.'

For a short while we sat in silence. A nurse appeared and told visitors it was time to leave.

'Mother,' I said quickly. 'Now don't get yourself into a panic, but I've got a bit of a problem. Do you think Uncle Olavi might be able to help me?' I told her about Arkady, the copies of the church registers and the whole complicated situation in which I now found myself.

Mother listened, raised her eyebrows quizzically and said she didn't have the energy to run around getting her grown sons out of trouble. Then she sighed melodramatically. 'But a mother is always a mother. I'll telephone Olavi. Let him contact you. It's safer that way.'

I drove back to the cottage. An elderly man walked by wearing a grey suit and a beret. I recognized him instantly, stopped the car and got out. 'Sir? Hello, how are you? Do you remember me?'

'Viktor Nikolayevich, what are you doing, careering round these parts? Come to see your poor cousins, have you? Or to cheer up your old mother? Though I heard you weren't always the apple of her eye – always up to tricks with Karpov's lad.' My former primary-school teacher Pavel Semyonov managed to sound like the same stern schoolmaster he'd been thirty years ago. He didn't wait for a response, but continued muttering.

I helped him into the car, remembering that he was the same age as my parents. This is what my father would have been like, had he still been alive, I thought. Or perhaps not; my father was a much bigger man. I recall him constantly belittling my teacher's enthusiasm for sports, saying the little man was trying in vain.

'Well, Vitya, you turned into an excellent skier after all, I could see it all those years ago. And your father was quite a fast one too – all you Finns are. When Nikolai set off, you could see his ski poles buckling in the middle as he propelled himself forwards. Nowadays the equipment is all made of plastic and glass fibre.'

'My skiing days ended when I was quite young. I didn't have it in me,' I interjected. 'But you seem to be in very fine fettle, sir. It's my mother I've come to see. She's had a heart attack, quite a serious one, but she looks like she'll pull through all right.'

My former teacher's next sentence remained unuttered. His mouth stopped open and his brow furrowed with sorrow. 'Dear me, I hadn't heard anything about it! I'll have to tell Nadya to visit, take her flowers or something. Dear oh dear, Nadya will be shocked to hear this. Goodness me.'

I dropped him off at the gate outside his house, which looked the same as always, but which seemed to have shrunk over the years. In the yard was the same old trestle with tires hanging from frayed strips of rope; a rusty old barbell and weights jutted up through the snow.

I watched as my teacher jogged the distance to the door and waved goodbye from the porch. The curtains quivered. His wife Nadya had been watching us from the window.

I returned to the car and felt glad that I'd been friendly to the old man. I recalled how Pavel Semyonov had been an enthusiastic member of the Party, how he had lectured the class about politics and made the pupils feel like sinful, unworthy future Communists. Now he was making do on a state pension barely more than a hundred marks a week – assuming it was ever paid on time – and looked on helplessly as his former students fled to Finland or turned to drink and prostitution. All that was left behind were the decrepit folks his own age and their rotting cottages. I used to imagine that when I grew up I would teach our schoolmaster a lesson and remind him of how he'd bullied us, how unfairly he'd treated us – but right now I wasn't in the mood to settle old scores.

That evening I drove to Riekkalansaari. The bridge was in bad condition. I had to wait for a Belarusian tractor heading into town to pull its wobbling trailer over the bridge before steering the Volkswagen across to the island.

I drove to an area of cottages where employees with the local factories and authorities had small cabins set on carefully toiled plots of land. I'd seen places like this in Finland too, but there they were called 'allotments'. The roads were ploughed, and many of the cottages were heated through the winter months.

I parked the car and walked the rest of the way. The cabin belonging to Lena's parents looked just as it had in the past; it was well looked after. I opened the gate into the garden and walked up the steps to the front door, which were covered in a layer of frozen snow. I peered into the veranda window, and through the lace curtains I saw the panelled walls, the varnished floorboards and furniture, the old guitar on the wall that I used to strum.

I sat on the steps. I recalled how Lena and I had come here from Leningrad, remembered the complicated train journey, our sandwiches, our walks along the edge of fields overgrown with a jungle of weeds and long grass. Lena was thrilled at the call of the corn crake and enjoyed identifying plants, shouting out their Latin names.

I remembered their place in Leningrad. It was a good apartment, in a good block; even its smell was dry and clean and warm. I would sit in the armchair reading a book I'd pulled from the shelves, which covered half the wall. Lena played her *études* over and over, agonizing over repeated passages, bit her nails to the quick and wiped tears from her eyes because her professor at the *conservatoire* – an old man with spectacles the lenses of which were like the glass found in old-fashioned flashlights – demanded nothing less than perfection. I remember him too, and I remember Lena wondering how I could sit listening to her 'boring playing': 'This isn't music; it's just notes, one after the other,' she sighed. I didn't understand the difference and I couldn't hear it, but I enjoyed sitting in the room with its high ceilings, the books and the whole warm, lazy afternoon.

Lena didn't understand or accept it when I said she was privileged. 'Me, the child of a middle-class family?' she would ask, aghast. I tried to explain what an enormous gap there was between being poor and being middle class, though in Soviet Russia such terms didn't exist – and therefore neither did the notion of class. Your own piano, your own bookshelf, a car and a *dacha,* fresh fruit on the table, foreign languages and friends abroad... None of this was Lena's fault or mine, but back then neither of us understood that.

The ring of my mobile phone brought me back to work matters and the search for Sirje Lillepuu.

'You're visiting family,' said Pervukhin, my contact in telecommunications. It wasn't so much a question as a statement of fact. 'I triangulated your phone for the fun of it. Anyway, that woman you were asking about: there have been no calls made from Sirje Lillepuu's phone for a few weeks. And except for you, nobody has tried to call her or leave her any messages. Besides, the phone has been completely switched off for the last few days, so I can't tell where it is.'

Before I could thank him, Pervukhin hung up. I stared at my phone and wondered what I ought to make of this information.

I had brought Sirje Larsson's case file with me, and now stared at my meagre collection of notes and the thin pile of photos. Aino Lillepuu had given me photographs of her daughter and made me swear to return them. She'd shown me Sirje's letters too, read them out loud, trying to translate into Finnish any sections I didn't understand. She had lowered her voice and told me all about her daughter: beautiful, worked hard at school, all in all a good girl.

Sirje had gone to college and started a secretarial course, but before long she'd taken a job with a firm looking after Estonian–Finnish trade, moved to Finland and decided to stay there. She had first met Aarne at work, then bumped into him later at a concert.

Sirje knew Aarne was married, but before long he'd filed for divorce, and she didn't put up much resistance when he eventually proposed to her. Aino Lillepuu told me that Sirje wasn't worried about not having children. She looked me in the eyes and said, with a sense of resignation, that she would probably never become a grandmother.

The more recent photograph Aarne Larsson had given me showed Sirje from the front, but the bunch of photographs her mother had handed me provided a much more three-dimensional view of her. Sirje always looked pretty, and there was something mysterious about her smile: she looked almost happy that she wasn't the centre of attention, but enjoyed watching others having fun. Most of the photographs were amateurish; the moments captured on film were slightly askew, the flash had rendered people's faces colourless and there was no depth to their smiles.

But there was one photograph that differed from the others. It was carefully composed according to the ideals of classical dimensions. Sirje was standing in the street, laughing, her white teeth showing. Her cheeks revealed a touch of colour from a trip to the south; light and shade lent her features character and depth. I recognized the location: the photograph had been taken on Lapinlahdenkatu, with the grey outline of Maria Hospital rising up behind her. I was convinced Esko Turunen must have taken the photograph.

I drove to the station to meet Alexei. I didn't go inside, or onto the platform, but waited in the car park. When I saw him in the station doorway I stepped out of the car so that he could see me. My brother was wearing a dark-brown suede jacket and a fur hat, and he had a large sports bag slung over his shoulder. We shook hands. When we were back in the car I noticed I was talking too much. Alexei listened, but for the most part he remained quiet, giving the occasional friendly chuckle; he said he was still getting used to hearing Finnish again after so long.

Back home we ate bread with sausage and pickled gherkins, and set off for the hospital. Mother was awake and took us both proudly by the hand. Her two boys. We sat on both sides of the bed. I left Alexei and Mother alone together, went home to get the sauna going, then picked my brother up from the hospital.

'I haven't had a sauna here for at least two years,' said Alexei as we sat sweating in the steam. He sat the way he had always sat there, on the upper bench, leaning against the back wall with both legs tucked up against his chest. I was used to thinking my brother was much older than me, that he looked much heavier and aged than I did. And when I walked past a mirror or window and saw my own reflection, I was often surprised to notice that I'd come to look very similar to him.

'If Mother dies, I'll have nothing left here,' said Alexei, and looked at me with his blue-grey eyes – familiar from my own mirror, too – and I realized the very same thing. Home would cease to exist. We would be alone. Orphans.

'Listen, little brother…' Alexei hesitated, then continued: 'What would you think if I moved to Finland? I've been thinking about it for a while.'

From the look of *faux* innocence on Alexei's face, I could tell he'd been thinking about it for more than a while. I threw water on the stove, forcing us to brace our heads against our knees as the steam leapt up from the burning stones towards the soot-covered walls and the old sauna boards that still wept with resin. *What about Irina and your son?* I wanted to ask. *What about the immigration papers? Have you thought about where to get a job or an apartment? Has it occurred to you that life in Finland isn't much easier than it is in Moscow?*

I inhaled the hot moisture in the air, cooled my head with water from the enamel pail and said simply: 'Of course I'll help you. But think carefully about what you want to do.'

We bathed together for a long time, occasionally adding logs to the fire beneath the stove, drinking beer and vodka and reminiscing about events from our childhood. We remembered things in different ways and almost got into an argument about whether or not I had been with the rest of the family watching a performance by Cossacks at the sports field.

'I remember the horses as clear as day. I remember the men jumping at speed from one horse to the next, and I remember what they were wearing. Besides, Uncle Eino was visiting that day, and he came to the show with us,' I said. Alexei eventually conceded that I probably had been there after all.

In the early hours my brother looked on the upper shelf of the wardrobe for his gleaming, red accordion, and found it exactly where he'd left it at least ten years earlier.

At first his fingers seemed stiff with age and lack of practice, but after a while he started playing surprisingly well. We sang together, Alexei in his Gypsy-flavoured tenor and me in my baritone. We sang old Soviet hits and Russian ballads in which the waters carried a straw like a careless love (or was it the other way round?) and where the wheat fields shimmered and the city lights dimmed.

And we wept together as we sang a nameless Finnish song our mother had taught us about a colourful bird feeding her fledglings while wind rocked the boughs of the trees.

15

The Mercedes from Ruuskanen's Quality Motors was waiting for me in the garage at Ruskeala. I took the keys and switched my Russian papers for the Finnish ones and left Igor Semyonov in his cardboard box to await new assignments.

At the border, the landscape seemed to change, turning neater and brighter as though spring were suddenly much further along. I drove south along Highway 6; the Mercedes' diesel motor ticked along nicely, and my speed picked up just as the thought of the work waiting for me in Helsinki came into mental focus. My number-one priority was Sirje Larsson, of whom I still hadn't found a trace.

At the Kouvola junction I turned west and reached Lahti by early afternoon. I looked among Aarne Larsson's papers for his first wife's address. The terraced house was easy to find.

I reclined the driver's seat further back and slouched there, almost horizontal, listening to an afternoon talk show on the radio and watching Helena Larsson's apartment. The street was so quiet that after half an hour I was worried I might draw attention to myself. People drove back from work, children were running off to their after-school activities, floor-ball sticks slung over their shoulders or riding helmets under their arms – but in Helena Larsson's apartment not even the curtains twitched.

I stepped out of the car and walked around the terrace. The small gardens were at the back of the building, and I would have needed a good pair of boots to get there in all the snow. I tried to look across the hedgerows as if I was minding my own business, but I knew I looked suspicious.

I walked back around to the front of the long terrace and rang Helena Larsson's doorbell. A low booming was coming from inside which, as doors opened inside the house, I recognized as bass-heavy metal music.

Kimmo Larsson looked vaguely like his father. Aarne's features were replicated in him, only they were softer, smaller and more delicate. The boy was scrawny and about my height. He had long hair, which he scooped away from his face with both hands. He stood with his shoulders hunched forward, his loose trousers scraped across the floor. He could have been anything at all – a junkie, a goth or a gospel guitarist. Perhaps not a hockey jock though, I concluded.

'Hello. I'm Viktor Kärppä from Helsinki. Your father Aarne has asked me to investigate the disappearance of Sirje Larsson. Is your mother Helena at home?'

'Mum's still at work or… out shopping or, whatever, I don't know. She should be back soon. Er, come on in.' The boy spoke clumsily, but in a surprisingly low, resonant voice. I wondered what kind of contralto his mother might be. His father's voice was metallic and grating and his son's voice was round, soft and grown-up. It was the kind of voice you could imagine coming from the throat of a much older, fatter man.

The hallway opened up into a dim, brown living room. I sat down in a springy armchair. The furniture might have been from the 1980s. The boy went to his room and turned the music down, then leaned against the bookshelves and didn't seem to know what to do with his hands. For a moment he held them against his chest, then let them dangle, calmly and unnaturally, at his sides.

Two similarly clad young men came out of the boy's room. In the hallway they pulled on their shoes, slung black trench coats over their shoulders and mumbled their goodbyes. In Russia, they would have shaken hands both with me and with one another, I thought; but, after all, back there so many things were so much worse than here.

'Me and Mum heard Sirje was missing. We weren't all that upset, but we weren't happy about it, either,' the boy suddenly said. 'Dad left us and took up with Sirje. It was a crap thing to do; it really sucked. But shit happens, right? Me and Mum haven't got anything to do with Sirje's disappearance.'

'I didn't suggest you did,' I said, trying to muster a tone of voice that implied I might just suspect something. 'When was the last time you saw your father and his new wife?'

'I was at their place in Helsinki just after Christmas. I came back to Lahti for New Year,' Kimmo said, forcing himself to appear calm and collected. I remembered the Larssons' house and their spare bedroom, which had about as much charm as a dentist's waiting room. I imagined his son would rather have been out drinking with his mates and seeing in the New Year than helping his father bind collectible books.

The front door rattled. I heard the sound of someone placing plastic bags on the ground followed by the jangle of keys; then the bags were carried into the kitchen. The fridge door opened, and the groceries were lifted into the cool air.

Helena Larsson walked into the living room and froze when she saw me. Her son turned and slunk off into his room without another word.

I propelled myself out of the armchair, greeted her and explained why I was there. 'Oh,' she replied with a lack of interest, then turned and took off her coat. A moment later she came back into the living room. Helena was wearing jeans and a checked flannel shirt. She was a good-looking woman with lively brown eyes, dark hair and the air of someone who takes good care of herself.

She sat down and pressed her hands against her cheeks, still cold from the outdoor air.

'The temperature's going to drop again overnight. When the sun sets,' she said with a smile. Her voice was pleasant, but bland. It seemed their son hadn't inherited his resonant vocal cords from either parent.

'I don't want to offend you or delve into painful subjects, but I'm looking into the disappearance of Sirje Larsson. I just spoke with Kimmo, but do you have any information that might help me, any ideas about what might have happened to her?'

'A detective, eh?' Helena smiled again. 'Aarne became immersed in the genealogy stuff and all that nonsense about related peoples in the late Eighties. It was a heated time, a time of liberation – politically I mean – and in Estonia too. After that he got carried away with the idea of another kind of liberation. And that's when he brought the immaculate Estonian back to be his bride...'

She sat silently for a moment, her hands in her lap.

'Of course, it hurt me. And it hurt Kimmo too, the rejection. But Aarne has always been a man of extremes, and I doubt our marriage would have lasted much longer anyway. Characteristics like those only grow over time – bigotry and stubbornness. I'm a more realistic and balanced person.'

She raised her eyes to look at me and continued in a mundane, colourless voice. 'Our marriage ended long before Sirje came into the picture. I didn't keep quiet about it – and certainly didn't accept it – but the truth is, he hit me.'

I froze, and a startled yelp jumped from my mouth. I hoped it hadn't sounded as though I was chuckling. I tried to correct it, and muttered that I was sorry to hear that. Helena cut off my bumbling attempt at sympathy and didn't seem to have taken offence. 'Aarne hit me once. That was enough.'

She started making some coffee. 'Yes please,' I said and thanked her. We continued talking about Aarne, their marriage and Sirje. Helena spoke gently and openly, and it was easy to believe her. The vague impression I'd had of Sirje came into focus, but Larsson's first wife's depiction didn't lend it any extra colour or shading.

'There's not much more to her, I'm afraid. Sirje is a pampered, innocent little girl from Tallinn. She'll soon be a middle-aged woman. She's happy with Aarne and her safe little life, the pretty house, the nice trips abroad. Apparently this is enough for Aarne too, though he's always been unsatisfied. At least, he was with me.'

Before leaving, I knocked once more on Kimmo Larsson's door and peered into his room. He had slipped out of the house without making a sound. The walls in his room were covered with posters of rock bands. Above his desk, attached to the wall with drawing pins, was a page from a newspaper with the headline in large, red lettering: ESTONIAN HOOKERS TAKING OVER HELSINKI STREETS.

It was doubtful that Aarne Larsson's former family had anything to do with Sirje's disappearance, but I began to suspect the threatening letter she had received might well have been written in this room.

16

I drove straight to the office, and had just switched on the computer when there was a knock at the window. Marja Takala gave a cautious wave and nodded shyly. I opened the door, trying to look professional, yet simultaneously happy and surprised to see her.

'Hi,' Marja said under her breath. For a moment she stood silently fidgeting with her scarf and looked like a lost Winnie the Pooh. 'I'm on my way to a party in Kallio, and thought I'd pop in and see how you were doing.' Again, she paused. 'I sent you an email but, I don't know, maybe you never got it or something...'

'I was out of town – in Sortavala, visiting my mother. She's quite ill. I've only just got back,' I explained in fragments, as though into a broken telephone. 'Are you in a hurry to get to your party? Take a seat – or we could go for coffee or something. I'll have time for work tomorrow, and I can read your messages then.'

But Marja had a plan, and it involved me. 'Well, I wondered whether you might like to come to the party *with* me. They are people I used to study with. It's only across the square on Toinen linja, really close.'

I quickly glanced over the post that had arrived at the office, switched off the computer and double-locked the door.

'Let's go via my apartment. I want to change clothes.'

'I don't know if I should, not with a Russian gangster like you,' Marja joked cautiously.

'That's right, Sortavala's very own sheriff. Frightening people and repossessing cars, that's my forte,' I smiled back – though I knew this was only half-true. Marja doubtless knew this too.

We stepped out the back door into the stairwell and walked across the empty courtyard. Marja was amused during our short journey in the rickety old lift: the warning sign had been defaced, its letters scraped away, and now read: CHILDREN UNDER TWELVE MUST BECOME ADULTS.

When we reached my apartment I apologized to Marja and stepped inside first. I picked up the accumulated newspapers, post and bills from the hallway floor and glanced around the apartment. It looked perfectly clean and fresh, though its inhabitant had been away for a week.

I showed Marja into the kitchen and hauled my suitcase onto the bed. My apartment was small, but it had a proper kitchen and a sizeable living room, next to which was an alcove large enough for a double bed. The bathroom was old-fashioned, but met my own standards of cleanliness.

I took some pickled gherkins and bite-sized pepperoni sausages from the fridge; apart from that, it was empty. In one of the cupboards I looked for some crackers, chocolate and vodka. I laid the offerings out on two small plates and poured us some vodka. We clinked our glasses.

'*Na zdorovie!* Welcome to my home.'

I shaved, but decided not to shower. 'What should I wear?' I shouted to Marja, who was in the kitchen.

'Nothing too fancy. You've seen what I'm wearing. Something like that,' she replied.

I guessed Ryshkov's wardrobe would only serve to heighten the elegant Russian-mafioso look. After giving the matter a moment's thought, I picked out a pair of black trousers, a black V-necked jumper and a grey jacket and dusted my shoes with a brush.

'That's smart enough.' Marja was standing in the living-room doorway. 'And the apartment is smart, too.'

Marja's eyes seemed to sparkle. 'Some of this stuff is totally retro, like the things you see in old photographs.' She walked around the apartment admiring the furniture, running her fingers across its surfaces. The coffee table and bookcase with the glass doors were made of varnished dark wood; the plain old sofa was upholstered in textured yellow-green fabric, and the green armchairs were in the same stylistic vein. I was particularly proud of my Rigonda Bolshoi stereo with its enormous set of Latvian speakers.

'It's trying to be the kind of living room I'd always imagined we might have at home. I pictured us living in Leningrad; my mother would be a teacher, and we would have everything you saw in photographs and on the television – a model Soviet home from the 1960s and 70s.' I tried to explain all this without making myself feel awkward. I trusted she would understand what I meant.

'Wow! I suppose you've got a Volga, and a Ural motorcycle, too? No, seriously, this is what nostalgia is all about. People miss things that were important when they were children, and try to recreate them.'

'I don't miss the Pioneers, or membership of the Komsomol,' I emphasized.

I decided not to mention that I did indeed have an old Volga waiting to be fixed in a corner of Ryshkov's garage in Vantaa. The statuette of the stag from its bonnet was currently standing on my desk in the office next to the bust of Lenin's head. Vladimir Ilyich sometimes ended up in a box, as he had a tendency to startle some of my clients. I wondered whether or not I should tell Marja about the Volga: its smell, its dial – the upper part of which was transparent, meaning that in the dark it shone blue light against the windscreen – and its tires filled with air from the Soviet Union.

'No, not directly, but you're living and recreating the values you were taught as a child,' Marja explained. 'The good things remain good. They are still worth trying to achieve.' I'd almost forgotten what she was referring to.

Marja Takala understood a surprising number of things. I imagined there were many things I could tell her about. I could tune the guitar and sing to her in Russian, so that all she could say was, 'Wow!'. But not quite yet.

I was clearly in the wrong place. The apartment on Toinen linja seemed full of loud students. In the living room, a few people were dancing in a sequence of strange jumps and gyrations, and in the kitchen people stood filling their glasses with red wine. On the dining table was salad in assorted serving bowls, broken pieces of baguette and a block of cheese wonkily sliced to one side. Smokers crushed next to one another on the balcony.

I managed to make out fragments of conversation, but they were so full of foreign terms nonchalantly bandied about that I couldn't quite keep up – or rather, that's precisely what I was doing, only a few words behind everyone else. I felt stupid, old and out of place.

Marja had introduced me to the few dozen guests at the party. Now she was mingling between clusters of friends with a glass of wine in her hand. Every now and then she looked over at me, and I raised my glass and tried to look as if I was enjoying myself. A few of the women politely came and chatted to me, and just as politely I tried to avoid any open flirtation, though I realized my presence had awoken a certain interest. They looked at me and assessed the situation, so that almost without thinking about it I drew a breath, tensed my chest muscles and stood up straight like a gymnast from yesteryear. Still, I tried to knock myself down again by thinking that they were only interested in me as an exotic guest who lived between countries.

I don't normally smoke, but now I had to come up with something to do, so I went out to the balcony. I managed to cadge a cigarette, leaned against the railing and looked out at the thousand and one windows of the Kallio municipal council building. A few of the windows were illuminated. I wondered why.

'So, how's our Russian friend?' a nondescript young man with glasses said by way of a hello. I didn't have time to answer before he launched into a lecture. 'It was a funny decision by President Koivisto to grant the Ingrians Law-of-Return status, don't you think? There are thousands of them here now, and the problems are getting worse all the time. There'll be no one left in Russian Karelia soon, as the smartest people – the Finns, that is – all want to come here.' Realizing his *faux-pas*, he added: 'Don't get me wrong, I don't mean they shouldn't have let *you* in.'

I got the impression he really did mean that people like me should be kept firmly on the other side of the border.

'I'm curious,' he said. 'Did you go to the army over there, and did you get into any trouble because you're not Russian? What nationality is indicated in your passport? Or was your father smart enough to get a Russian passport and live as a good, upstanding citizen? A Party member, maybe?' The man raved on: 'You hear stories about Russian prisons and the army, things about how they treat anyone that isn't Russian. Bullying, hazing, screwing them in the ass, that sort of thing.'

He reminded me of Vassily Solovyov, a man who had moved from Bukhara to Leningrad to study and ended up living in our four-person dorm. When he was drunk, he regularly got into scrapes. He would walk up to some bruiser in the street and start mouthing off at him: 'Dumb-looking asshole…' Vassily would keep on and on so long that even the calmest of big men would eventually clock him square in the face. After that, Vassily would gather up his belongings and carry on muttering under his breath: 'Only a dumb asshole hits a smaller man…' Solovyov was a liability to himself, and so was this wiseass.

'I've never been in prison, either in Russia or in the Soviet Union,' I replied, trying to sound clipped and to the point. 'My passport says I'm a *Finka*, a Finn, and so did my father's. And yes, he was a probationary member of the Party. I did just under two years of military service, and the rest I served as part of my studies. University students are either reprieved altogether or required to attend special courses. That's what I did.'

I didn't want to be the dumb asshole who punched men smaller than him. Looking at the guy, I guessed he must have weighed about 60 kilos to my 90. I leaned closer to his face.

'In the barracks, there are two types of men. There are guys who fuck you in the ass, and there are guys who get fucked *in* the ass. You see, it's like the theory of relativity. Both guys are getting screwed, but one of them is – relatively speaking – better off. Well, whatever floats your boat.'

'Jesus Christ, the Russian here's getting a bit fruity,' said the guy in the glasses, angry now.

The smokers on the balcony watched us from a distance. The man was thinking of what to say or do next. He suddenly decided to grab his beer bottle and try to hit me. I ducked, struck him across the wrist with the palm of my hand, grabbed his left arm and yanked it behind his back. I pushed him against the railing, twisting his wrist with one arm and pulling up the back of his trousers with the other, forcing him over the edge.

'I've got a lot of sympathy for the owner of that Nissan down there, so I'm not going to throw you on its roof. You'd accelerate at a rate of 9.81 metres per second. The canopy on the second floor won't break your fall much, and the airbags won't be any use either,' I whispered into his ear. 'Now, I'm going to lift you back onto the balcony and you're going to take it nice and easy, right? We'll both laugh about it, everybody will think we were just fooling around and you won't look like an idiot. Got it?'

The man in spectacles nodded vehemently, and I pulled him back over the railing. He was trembling, but tried to laugh it off. 'Jesus, Kärppä, that was fun. I need another drink.' He disappeared inside the apartment.

Marja was standing at the balcony door and stepped next to me. We turned and leaned against the railing. She sipped her wine and pursed her lips – but not because of the wine.

'Was that really necessary? Ilkka is always like that when he's pissed. Don't pay him any attention. Or do you always behave like a gorilla?' Her words sounded like a direct accusation, and her dark eyes were looking right at me.

'No, but you realize these people treat me as if I were one. They talk the most ridiculous nonsense and don't care the least bit about other people. "Oh really," they say, if I say something I think is quite smart, making sure to sound as condescending as possible, as though I'd said something utterly stupid, then continue talking about something else. It's probably best if people like me stick to doing the cleaning.'

Marja didn't say a word. She slipped her hand underneath my coat and gently rubbed my back, her fingers drawing soft figures of eight, her touch so gentle that I was imagining the patterns more than feeling them.

'I get it, but I don't excuse it. It's natural that you see things from your own perspective, but you can't throw someone off the balcony if he says something that annoys you. Besides, nobody here has had much time to belittle you yet.'

Marja looked pensive. She paused again, then smiled. 'Did you think you had to prove to me what a man you are? Remember, I'm an emancipated, modern woman. That kind of testosterone machismo doesn't have any effect on me.'

I looked her in the eyes; her pupils had widened in the darkness. 'I'm old enough to know it does have an effect. Or would you rather take some kind of librarian to a party?'

'Don't make fun, or I might just do that next time. And what have you got against librarians?'

17

We walked along the side of the Hakaniemi market hall. Marja stopped and looked at me. 'The metro isn't running anymore, and the buses can be pretty packed at this time of night. I could stay at your place.'

'I think I can manage that. I'll make up the sofa for you,' I said, feigning seriousness. I hadn't had time to get all emotional about it when a white Volkswagen Golf pulled up in front of us, on the pavement.

'Well, Kärppä, you're quite the ladies' man,' Detective Inspector Korhonen said through his open window. Parjanne was in the driver's seat. I told Marja that these two jokers were buddies from the police sports club, and asked her to wait to one side.

'That's right, Viktor here's partial to a spot of floor ball,' Korhonen chuckled. 'Hey, Viktor, you should know this one: what is it your brothers are called, again? It's easy, it's written on the front of a Marlboro packet: *Veni, Vidi, Vici*.'

Korhonen stepped out of the car, grabbed my arm and pulled me over to the market wall.

'I know Karpov got screwed out of a million marks' worth of Marlboros, or whatever *makhorka* knock-offs they were. And I suppose you should know Yura Koshlov was chopped to pieces in a kiddies' sandpit near a motel in Lapinjärvi. A local hooker told me she'd seen the killers at the petrol station washing blood off their shoes, packing body parts into plastic bags and stashing them in the boot of their car. But you can bet those guys aren't in town any more, and if they ever come back they'll be new men. The tart's not around any more either; she's had a change of career.'

Korhonen gripped my jacket and pulled me so close I could feel the warmth of his breath on my face and the smell of food and tobacco in my nostrils.

'I paid Jaak Lillepuu a little visit, told him I knew he'd taken out Koshlov and stolen the smokes,' Korhonen hissed. 'He laughed in my face and blew smoke in my eyes. He knows I've got nothing on him, not a fucking shred of evidence. People tell me all kinds of things, but none of them will turn up in court to testify. Now, shrug your shoulders and make it look like I've been asking you a few questions. Parjanne doesn't need to know what we're up to. But for your information, and just so you know, it was Lillepuu. Straight up.'

Korhonen let go of me; I straightened my jacket and walked back to where Marja was standing. The police officers' Golf drove along the edge of the pavement, its chassis scraping across the curb as Parjanne steered it back onto the road.

Korhonen hollered out the window: 'Here's a good one. You know what, honey, I wouldn't waste my time with Kärppä – he's a bit of a "Red" herring. Get it?' He was still laughing at his own dumb joke as they rounded the corner of the market.

'What was *that* all about?' asked Marja, somewhat stunned.

'They're just showing off,' I explained glibly, and took her hand.

Once we had walked to the edge of the square I saw a dark BMW parked outside my office. I pulled Marja closer, and we changed direction so that we walked in front of the closed hotdog stand at the end of the square.

'I suppose this is as romantic a place as any,' she said.

'Listen, this is serious,' I said gravely. 'And when I say it's serious, I mean it. There's a car parked outside my office; if I'm right, inside that car are three Estonian guys. They've probably already been inside my apartment and worked out that I've gone off somewhere, though my car is still parked downstairs. Now they're waiting for me to come home again. I don't think they're out to kill me, not here at least. But they're up to something – and they've got plans for me.'

I twisted two keys free from my key ring. 'Take these and go in through the gate into house number six. Walk around the building, go into the stairwell and up to the landing in the attic and wait for me there. Don't go into the apartment. If you get into trouble, those keys will get you into any stairwell in the block. If you don't hear from me in half an hour, call Korhonen, the police officer we just saw. I'll give you his number.'

Marja gave a curt nod. She didn't ask any questions and didn't ask me to repeat the instructions. She keyed Korhonen's number into her phone.

'I'll come and get you. And in case you were wondering, my life isn't normally like this,' I tried to reassure her flippantly. Marja walked off and smiled a pale goodbye.

I crossed the square and headed towards the large trade-union building opposite, and wondered whether I was in trouble up to my knees or my neck. No matter, it seemed like the water levels were rising around me. Three men were sitting in the warm car waiting for me, and they would wait as long as it took, until I either came home or went to the office. I might as well confront them right away.

I walked by the trade-union building, past the taxi rank on the corner, and headed towards Merihaka. I advanced a few hundred metres then turned back, and as I approached Viherniemenkatu I pressed myself tight against the wall. At the corner I took a deep breath, knelt down and carefully peered round into the street.

The BMW was waiting quietly in its parking spot with the engine switched off. They must keep the engine on sometimes, I thought, otherwise the car would get cold and the windows would steam up. My Volvo was parked at the front of a row of cars at this end of the street; behind it was a Toyota, and after that the BMW.

In the boot of the Volvo was my gun.

I crept back behind the wall, took out my phone and searched for the number of the city taxi service. There were no cabs waiting outside the union building, and the call was transferred to the switchboard. I asked for a car to pick me up at Viherniemenkatu 6.

'Order number 614. Thank you,' said the nameless woman at the other end.

A Nissan with a diesel engine arrived within five minutes. It turned at the end of the street and stopped a car's length in front of the BMW.

Shielded by the Nissan and keeping my head down, I dashed behind my Volvo, opened the lock and held the boot ajar just wide enough to slip my hand inside. I hoped the light from the boot wouldn't show up in the BMW's rear-view mirror. I groped around for the tool bag next to the spare tire, pulled a cloth bag from inside it, took it out and gently closed the boot again. Inside the bag was a

Chinese copy of a large German SIG Sauer pistol. It was a good, cheap weapon.

Still keeping my back down, I walked close up against the row of parked cars until I reached the BMW, then yanked open the door on the driver's side. Jaak Lillepuu turned and looked right down the dark barrel of the pistol.

'Evening,' I said. 'How's it going? Tell your boys to get in that taxi, go to the stadium and watch a match. You and I are going to have a little chat. Either that, or at the very least you'll be needing a dentist. My hand's already twitching, my finger's going to cramp any minute.'

Lillepuu looked at the pistol and at me in turn. His eyes seemed crooked as he tried to focus on the barrel of the gun pressing against the corner of his mouth. I wasn't laughing. Lillepuu's henchmen had frozen in a Napoleon pose: both had slipped their hands beneath their jackets to reach for their holsters.

'Right, lads, get into the taxi and drive to the petrol station near the zoo,' Lillepuu said in Finnish. 'I'll meet you there. Kärppä isn't going to kill me.' He added: 'We weren't going to kill you either.' It sounded like he was explaining this as much to his own men as he was to me. The pair slowly removed their hands from their jackets and walked towards the taxi, their arms unnaturally stiff. A cloud of sooty fumes puffed from the back of the Nissan as it pulled away.

'Well?' I tried to prompt Lillepuu. I sat down in the back seat, making sure he could see my weapon at all times. Lillepuu remained in the driver's seat and kept his hands on the steering wheel where I could see them.

'We thought we'd pay you a visit and remind you what we talked about on the boat. I've got my own business affairs, and you can keep your nose out of them. Concentrate on finding Sirje. I'll hire you to get to the bottom of it. You see, I can't… I mean, if something comes up, I can't just go to the police and tell them about it, or they'll twist things and use them against me.'

'Thanks, but I only have one paying customer per case. And in this case it's Larsson.'

Lillepuu was quiet for a moment. 'That's good. Concentrate on him. That's where you'll find the truth, if you get my drift.'

He turned to look at me, careful to keep his hands on the steering wheel all the while. He didn't seem afraid, though the barrel of my pistol was only an inch from his nose. I slowly edged back from him, slammed the door shut and backed away from the BMW. Lillepuu started the ignition and glided off. The tires didn't screech, and he didn't look behind him; he gradually accelerated until all that was left of the BMW was a cloud of exhaust and the rumbling of his motor.

I walked up the staircase, trying to make my footsteps sound carefree and natural. I quietly called out to Marja. She peered out at me through the banister on the upper floor.

'I don't think I've ever been so afraid,' she said, agitated. 'Who were those men, and what have you done?'

'I'm still looking for the missing Estonian girl, and her brother is some kind of small-time crook. He doesn't like me asking around about his business,' I explained. I took Marja by the hand and rubbed her fingers. 'I was more worried you might have disappeared. It takes much less than that to scare most people.'

'How could I have disappeared? I was frozen with worry. Dammit, Kärppä!'

Extra bonus points for Marja Takala.

I had a dream that night:

I am back at primary school. It's an art class; we're drawing a forest in charcoal. I draw a picture of a spruce. I brag about being able to make the needles and branches look natural. Then, suddenly, I'm no longer able to draw them, and the trees look like brown cacti. The teacher comes over to help me. She's a young woman, and wears a blue suit with a brown brooch on her chest, her hair puffy and backcombed. The teacher has the face of Sirje Larsson. At the back of the classroom, in the bad boy's seat, sits Jaak Lillepuu. He barely fits behind his desk. 'You broke my watch, and you're going to pay for it,' he whispers to me. I can smell his bad breath, see his broken teeth. I'm frightened.

I jolted awake. Marja had taken the duvet, wrapped herself inside it into a tight, warm bundle. That night she'd laughed at my Russian duvet covers, into which you have to slip the duvet from a square-shaped opening in the side. She wouldn't believe my explanations of how ingenious a design it was, though I reminded her that Russians have been flying around in space for decades.

I was now wide awake, lucid. The clock told me it was half past five, and the sounds of the early-morning city could be heard outside. I snuggled against Marja. We were like two spoons in a drawer, one cupped around the other. I slid my arm beneath the curve of her body and pulled her towards me, keeping one hand on her chest and one on her hip. Marja felt my body and my embrace in her sleep, but didn't wake. She didn't resist; instead, she pressed her hip against me. My mind clouded over. Was all this so familiar to her that she didn't think twice when someone slept close to her?

I pressed my eyes shut and repeated to myself that I would soon fall asleep. I wanted to wake up next to Marja again, this time my head full of lighter, more pleasant thoughts.

18

Even the memory of snow eventually melted beneath piles of grit and in the corners of shady gardens. Street-cleaning vans buzzed along like early-morning wasps, whipping up dust along the streets of Helsinki. I felt immensely relaxed, despite the image in my mind's eye of that perfect worker, the record-setting Soviet miner Stakhanov, sitting on my shoulder and reminding me occasionally of all my unfinished work – particularly in the case of Sirje Larsson. Aarne Larsson had paid me handsomely – at least a month's wages – but so far the results of my investigation weren't much to write home about.

Mother had been allowed home. After much discussion, Alexei and I had convinced her to allow a cleaner into the house once a week. Karpov's men promised to bring her groceries regularly, and to make sure there was always enough firewood in the shed.

Alexei and I spoke on the phone. He was still in Sortavala, and about to get the train back to his life in Moscow, a thousand kilometres away. He didn't mention his plans to move back to Finland, and I didn't ask.

'Listen, Viktor, it was really great to see you and talk. I hope we can meet up... before we need to organize the funeral,' he said, trying to avoid the subject of the inevitable.

Mother's illness had been a bigger blow to my brother than to me. He didn't want to speak about death. Even Mother had had enough of it, and now she seemed to want to take care of all the arrangements in her own level-headed way. She had planned a small funeral, told us where she'd hidden all her account books in the dresser – *what value can all those old roubles possibly be,* she'd laughed – and had reserved her plot next to Father in the graveyard. She reminded us that a grave doesn't have any sentimental value, and said we didn't need to erect a temple there or plant flowers.

There was another call I had to make to Sortavala, this time on an even more serious matter. I walked across the square to the kiosk, bought a phone card, looked for a phone booth and keyed in Karpov's number.

'Hello?'

I didn't introduce myself, and kept it brief. 'It's a done deal. The smokes, the missing "C" and the rest of it. It's Jaak Lillepuu.'

'You must have the wrong number, friend,' Karpov replied. 'Don't know what you're talking about.'

I tore up the phone card and disposed of the pieces in different litterbins. I wasn't planning on claiming it in my tax declaration, either. My friends and employers changed phone cards regularly, but you still had to watch your mouth. I imagined the police stations employed legions of men whose job it was to sit in a closed room with headphones on their ears, listening in to phone conversations and isolating snatches of information. And when you were turning in evidence to a court martial that only dealt in death penalties, you had be extremely vigilant.

Stakhanov whispered Sirje's name once more, and again I went through the motions. I contacted my network, but didn't come up with anything new about her or Lillepuu. I asked around about any connections with Sweden and put out the word among the Estonian circles in Stockholm. If Sirje had gone west, I believed I'd soon find out about it.

There were a few things to be getting on with besides Sirje. I wrote and translated some paperwork for Ruuskanen's tax-free car deals – shipments of Mercedes, BMWs and Audis were being brought from Germany to Finland and moved on directly to Russia – and supervised two unauthorized deliveries of coloured scrap metal at Kotka harbour. Gennady Ryshkov sent an entrepreneur to my office, and I was to help him draw up a set of duplicate invoices. For the tax and customs authorities we compiled one set of documents, while the true value and cost of transportation was on another set of papers altogether.

I did the job cash-in-hand, and without a receipt. There was no proof that Viktor Kärppä ever got up to anything illegal. And when he did, it certainly wasn't cheap.

The most hardened criminal I dealt with in the following days was one Vitaly Ponomaryov, a professional hockey player from Chelyabinsk who now lived in Espoo. He spoke only Russian; this was the first winter he'd spent abroad. Ponomaryov had been trying to get in touch with his Finnish–Russian agent but, when he couldn't get hold of him, he called me instead.

'I'm in real trouble,' Ponomaryov explained, and I could hear from his voice that he was scared. 'A couple of guys turned up at my door. They showed me some kind of ID and demanded to see my documentation. The next night the doorbell rang, and through the peephole I saw two soldiers. I didn't dare open the door.'

I tried to calm the defenceman, who was known for his aggressive playing style – but now he was in a panic. I told him I knew he had all the right documentation and work permits, that he'd paid his taxes and that his rent wasn't in arrears. Everything should be fine and dandy. I promised I'd look into the matter.

I called the hockey club and the Espoo police department, hunted down Ponomaryov's agent and finally went to his house and talked to his neighbours. The hockey player lived in the district of Matinkylä. I found him at home.

'Relax, Vitaly,' I tried to assure him. 'The guys asking for documentation were TV licence inspectors. The club promised to take care of it. You've got a television, right?'

Ponomaryov nodded.

'As for the soldiers, turns out they were a couple of young recruits collecting money for veterans.'

I took the Länsiväylä highway back into Helsinki, turned off towards Kamppi and stopped at the red lights outside the Forum shopping mall. Pedestrians were winding their way across the street and into the mall, and in the crowd I spotted a dark-haired woman. In truth, what I saw wasn't really a figure, but more a flash of colour and shape. I didn't so much see her face as sense it, and glimpsed her profile as she walked away from me. I revved the engine, steered the Volvo up onto the pavement, slapped the sign MAINTENANCE – KETOLA ELECTRICS on the dashboard and hurried after the woman.

There must have been about a hundred people in the entrance hall of the shopping mall, going up, down, left and right, towards me, away from me, around me. I tried to assess the situation calmly, glance across one section at a time to see if I could find that short, red jacket and dark head of hair. My eyes picked out a local football shirt, a red woolly hat and scarf in the window of a fashion outlet and advertising slogans in red lettering – until, finally, I spotted the woman getting off the escalator on the floor above.

I dashed after her, shoving people out of my way, apologizing as I went, *sorry, sorry,* and ran up the stairs. I saw the woman in the plaza above. She was crouching down, looking in the window of a sports shop, sale posters screaming in capital letters behind her. I slowed my pace to a gentle jog. 'Sirje,' I said quietly, and gently touched her shoulder. The woman didn't shout or scream. She simply moved away and gave me a puzzled look. She was beautiful; but she was not Sirje Larsson.

'I'm sorry… I thought you were someone else. Sorry.' I stepped away and walked back to the car. I decided to pay Esko Turunen a little visit.

Pedestrians gave me angry, irritable looks as I steered the Volvo off the pavement and back onto the road. I drove along Mannerheimintie, turned at Lönnrotinkatu, wound my way through the small side streets and reached Lapinlahdenkatu. I parked the car and took out my satchel. I only had to wait ten minutes until the front door opened and the same girl as before stepped out, the same sour expression on her face. I said 'hi' as though she were an old friend, and the girl muttered something in reply. This time her hair wasn't in a bun, but held together with a complex combination of clips and pins.

I stepped into the courtyard and saw that the lights were on in Esko Turunen's apartment. I slowly took the stairs up to the third floor and listened to the door with my stethoscope once again. I could hear music and the sound of footsteps getting louder. I moved back, startled and worried that someone was about to come out of the apartment, open the door outward into my face and ask awkward questions about my equipment; but after the footsteps came a loud splashing, a toilet flushing and the sound of someone washing their hands.

I gave the doorbell a lively ring. I rang it again. I waited ten seconds and rang a third time. Then I pressed my ear against the door and listened with the stethoscope. Turunen was up to his old tricks again.

For a while I sat in the corridor, waiting. From the courtyard I'd seen that the window in Turunen's apartment was open. From the balcony in the stairwell, it was only about a metre or so up to the window ledge. At first glance it didn't seem like too acrobatic a stunt, though I wasn't very enthusiastic about it. I don't like high places; I've never understood the attraction of tall buildings or death-defying fairground rides. But needs must. I took a deep breath and quietly slipped out onto the balcony.

I was grateful for the evening darkness. Nobody glancing up at the building would see me; the streetlights were all angled towards the doors and bins. I gripped the ventilation pipe, gave it a tug and tried hanging from it to check that it would take my weight. It survived a chin-up. From my satchel I took a length of rope and tied it to the railing. I wrapped the rope round my left arm, tied it in a loose knot behind my back and the rest I coiled round my right hand before clambering onto the railing. I tried to concentrate on staring up at Turunen's window, leaned my weight on the rope and swung my leg up to the side, just the way I'd learned years ago in the Soviet army. I slipped my leg onto the window ledge, yanked hard on the rope, hauled myself upright and grabbed the middle bar of the window frame.

It was an old-style ventilation window of the open-and-closed type. It reminded me of some of the designs I'd had to interpret when working as a carpenter's apprentice, when I first moved to Finland. I opened the latches and just managed to slide through the gap. I found myself in the kitchen. The chair beneath the window was in an awkward position, and I had to balance on one leg. The kitchen was clean and empty. The dining table had been cleared, the wax-cloth covering wiped clean, and there were no dishes left on the draining board.

I walked into the living room, where I found Esko Turunen standing in the middle of a red-striped rug wearing black trousers and a black shirt.

'You must not have heard me ring the bell,' I said, trying to muster the austere voice of a debt collector as best I could.

Turunen stood up straight, and only then did I see that he was a big man. A really big man. It wasn't only that he was tall – well over six feet – but he was thick-set, bulky, heavy-built, powerful… Everything about him was strong and massive without being remotely fat. His build and proportions made him look like an overgrown baby Jesus painted in the manner of a Pre-Raphaelite master.

I already regretted my entrance and abrasive opening line. Turunen could crush me with his bare hands, rugby-tackle me against the wall and throw me right back out the window

– the larger window, if I was lucky enough. There was no way to backtrack, to soften the impression I'd already made by adding a few friendly conditionals and polite wishes. The giant started to speak.

'Can't you people just leave me in peace? I've already told you countless times, I don't know where Sirje is. She's my friend, that much is true, we talk about much more than painting, but there's nothing else going on between us. Sirje is a quiet girl, she wouldn't get involved in anything untoward. And neither would I, for that matter.'

Turunen stood stock still, his feet facing slightly inwards, holding his hands together in front of him. He spoke faintly, almost whispering, and his voice had a distinctive Helsinki nasal quality, and his sharp lisping 'S' made him seem all the more like an overgrown child. I stepped a little closer. Turunen was startled, and instinctively raised his hands as if to protect his abdomen. The thumb, forefinger and middle finger on his right hand were taped together; white bandages and a splint covered his hand. I guessed the support ran half way up his forearm.

'Hey, take it easy,' I said, trying to calm him down. I continued talking almost out of friendship and solidarity, wanting to reassure him. 'My name's Viktor Kärppä, and I'm trying to track down Sirje Larsson. She's missing, and her husband, parents and brother are all beside themselves with worry. But I'm not about to do any harm to Sirje or you. I'm not an Estonian gangster. I've been hired to look for Sirje.'

Turunen stared at me long and hard. I tried to look as calm and as trustworthy as a real-estate dealer who smiles at a hesitant client as if to say, *There's no rush, there's plenty of time to think it over* when all you want to say is, *Just buy the fucking place or complain about the floorboards elsewhere; I've got another viewing in fifteen minutes and those signs aren't going to carry themselves.*

He looked at me again, trying to make sense of everything. 'I know. I've had people round here asking about her.' He raised his hand and showed me his bandaged fingers. 'Jaak Lillepuu was actually quite polite, though Sirje had warned me about her brother's reputation before. Aarne Larsson did this to me.'

19

I was in Pakila, sitting in an Opel Vectra that I'd borrowed from Ruuskanen's yard. The day before I'd been following Aarne Larsson's movements in a borrowed Renault. Larsson had closed his shop on the dot of six o'clock; I'd followed his Saab back to Pakila and spent a long evening outside his home, watching his non-existent movements. At least, to me they seemed non-existent. Larsson switched on the lights when he came home and switched them off again just before midnight.

It looked like this evening wasn't going to be much livelier. Marjatta Nyqvist left the neighbouring house to go for a run with her Irish setter, with which I was now familiar, but I decided not to say hello to her and slid instead further down behind the Opel's dashboard so she wouldn't see me. I wondered how it was possible that all the other residents remained stubbornly indoors.

Even out here you could follow the change in television programmes through the windows. Lights flickered in sync with one another, and I tried to recall the most popular programmes on different channels. The children's rooms went dark before ten o'clock; parents fetched supper from the kitchen; and, in a surprising number of houses, everyone went to bed by eleven. Larsson switched his lights out at the same time as he had the previous night.

My encounter with Esko Turunen had told me at least as much about Sirje as I'd learned from my trips to Pakila and Tallinn. I believed that things were just as Turunen had assured me: he and Sirje were good friends, nothing more. Sirje had always been shy and quiet, almost socially inhibited, but she had opened up to Turunen, telling him about her childhood, her school years and her marriage.

He didn't believe that Sirje had run away, or that she was trying to escape something or someone. Sirje didn't want to be anywhere else, didn't dream of adventure. He admitted that Aarne Larsson was a strict man, and that he didn't care much for oil painting or any other esoteric nonsense. But he was Sirje's husband, and Sirje didn't regret her marriage.

Sirje had missed a few lessons. Turunen called her, but Aarne had answered and said she wasn't at home. Soon afterwards, Aarne paid Turunen a visit, telling him that Sirje was missing and almost accusing him of having something to do with it. When Turunen had tried to assure him he knew nothing of her disappearance, Aarne had called him a poof, a clown and a good-for-nothing, and twisted Turunen's hand so forcefully that he'd had to go to the doctor, where he claimed he'd fallen over and was given two weeks' sick leave. He worked as a clerk with a courier company, he explained. You can't sort shipments or sign for deliveries with torn ligaments.

Turunen seemed relieved at being able to tell me this. Jaak Lillepuu had visited him, too, but seemed satisfied upon hearing that Turunen hadn't seen Sirje for weeks. I didn't consider myself particularly sympathetic, but compared to Jaak Lillepuu I imagined must have seemed like a benevolent

Jehovah's Witness turning up at the door. Turunen couldn't say why Aarne Larsson had become so violent. Aarne knew perfectly well the pair weren't having an affair. Perhaps he was simply on edge from all the worry, Turunen suggested. I wondered the same thing. There was something about Esko, something weak and vulnerable, something that was easy to hurt, to bully.

I'd had enough of staring at Larsson's sleepy house, and was just reaching for the keys in the ignition when, in the rear-view mirror, I saw a shiny black car gliding along the street. I slid further down, trying to make myself invisible behind the seat and the headrest. The BMW coasted past Larsson's house, did a U-turn a hundred metres away and waited on the street next to a grey Peugeot. A man's head craned out the window and seemed to be chatting in the direction of the Peugeot. I opened my own window a little but couldn't make out anything above the familiar hum of the motor.

The BMW slowly pulled away, and continued past Larsson's house without stopping. In the mirror I saw the flicker of its brake lights at the end of the road and the traffic lights flashing amber. Then the car gently accelerated towards Tuusulantie. The Peugeot remained parked on the street. I waited.

At around two o'clock I saw the driver of the Peugeot. He stepped out of the car and stretched his limbs, stiff from all the sitting. He took a piss at the corner of the hedgerow, and then, with his hands in his pockets, walked past Larsson's house and past me until he reached the end of the road; then he turned back again. The man seemed relaxed and carefree, like a car thief looking for his next prey. Only the whistling was missing. I wondered whether or not he knew I was staking out the house. I hadn't noticed him, and he hadn't necessarily seen me either.

I didn't recognize him as one of Lillepuu's henchmen. Average height, blue jacket and polo-necked jumper, jeans, dark hair, an earring, no beard. He returned to his Peugeot and set off. At the intersection he, too, turned in the direction of the motorway.

It didn't bother me if the Estonians knew I was keeping an eye on Larsson; after all, Lillepuu had all but encouraged me to do so. But I was perplexed as to why Jaak Lillepuu wanted to stake out his own sister's house.

20

The following morning, I set off to Kouvola in the early hours on an errand for Ryshkov. The Volvo's studded tires screeched against the dry asphalt, but I enjoyed driving, enjoyed whistling to the radio and talking to Marja. I'd invited her to accompany me, and it had taken her all of five seconds to decide whether to join me for a day out in the countryside or stay at home preparing her seminar presentation. (The subject had something to do with Bolshevik feminism, and although I imagined I knew a thing or two about the everyday nature of the subject, I decided to keep my mouth well and truly shut.)

Once on the road, I telephoned my mother. She gushed about the crocuses blossoming at the side of the house, though there was still a cold wind blowing in across Lake Ladoga.

When we arrived in Kouvola I drove to the railway station, where we took the tunnel up to one of the middle platforms. A dozen or so other people were waiting for the morning train from St Petersburg. An old acquaintance waved and said hello. He was originally from the village of Kharlu, but had later moved to Finland. He gripped my hand with both of his, then held Marja's between his warm fists for a long time and enveloped us with his gentle, singsong accent. I'd helped him and his wife during their move, and to settle in Finland. The couple now lived in Kuusankoski; they were waiting at the station for his wife's sister, who was paying a visit. In just a few minutes, the old man managed to fill me in on how all his children and grandchildren were getting on.

The old Repin train arrived on time. Once it came to a halt the platform filled with neatly dressed Finnish businessmen, young Russian men in leather jackets, women in headscarves and chubby old gentlemen. A short man in a fur hat had a slab-shaped package wrapped in brown paper tucked under his arm, and in his free hand he was carrying a small, fake-leather suitcase. I greeted him curtly, and he carefully placed the package on the ground. We shook hands; I picked up the package, and we both walked off towards the car park.

Marja sat in the back. I put the package and suitcase in the boot and opened the passenger-side door for the man. He only reached for his seatbelt once I pointed out that, in Finland, wearing a seatbelt wasn't a matter of choice. I kept an eye on the traffic in the car's mirrors and tried to see whether or not anyone was tailing us.

I drove into the forecourt outside the Vaakuna Hotel. The taciturn Russian expressed dismay at the building's pink façade, but seemed to take my word for it when I said it would hardly keep him awake at night. In accordance with Ryshkov's instructions, I gave him a grand in cash. He thanked me and said he knew what to do with it. We stepped out of the car and said goodbye, and I handed him his suitcase and brown package from the boot.

'Is that it?' Marja asked, somewhat incredulous, as I pulled out of the hotel car park. 'I mean, is that the reason you had to leave Helsinki so early this morning, just so you could chauffeur some old man to a hotel in Kouvola?'

'That's one thing I've never understood about life in Finland: nobody takes proper care of the elderly,' I commented with *faux* indignation, and drove towards the intersection of Highway 6 at Kuusankoski.

'Okay,' I continued, 'you don't need to know this, but I might as well tell you because you've already seen one thing and another. That man is a fairly good artist, but his abstract paintings don't really sell in Helsinki or St Petersburg. So instead, he paints landscapes of the shores of Lake Ladoga, the Valamo monastery, the old town in Vyborg and so on, and sells them at flea markets in Finland. He makes a decent living from it, too.'

'But what does that have to do with you?'

'Well, hidden beneath his landscapes, or in amongst the other paintings, are really valuable art and icons. Ryshkov has a couple of clients who order them. They either end up on the walls of private penthouses in Töölö or go to auction.'

'So is he taking them to Helsinki tomorrow? And why did you have to pay him for them?'

'His package of paintings is now in the boot of the car. I already had an identical package full of paintings for the flea market, which might have been the paintings in which the genuine art was brought into the country. These new paintings I'll now take to Ryshkov.'

I drove towards Lahti as Marja slowly took all this in. 'But smuggling valuable art is really wrong. And where did the icons come from?' she asked disapprovingly.

'From people's homes. Heathens inherit holy effigies from deceased relatives and sell them on. Some are from Valamo,

Konevitsa and other churches across Russia,' I explained. 'There's no shortage of churches in Russia, believe me, and they're not going to run out of icons any time soon. And you can get other kinds of art from museums, if you've got the money. You don't necessarily need all that much either. Call it privatization, if you will. Of course it's wrong, but in order to get by people will sell anything they've got or anything they can get their hands on.'

We drove on in silence for a while, but then Marja snapped: 'Okay, so some people over there steal because they're starving. Fine. But you and Ryshkov aren't starving. You're the ones making money out of this scam.'

'Listen, I never said I was some kind of Robin Hood. I've thought about these things too, and I'm sure my mother would have fewer grey hairs and a healthier heart if I'd ended up taking a job as an engineer at Nokia or a farmer in Karelia; but things didn't work out like that. Not in Leningrad, not in Sortavala, and not here in Finland, either. I'm not complaining, and I don't want to blame anybody, but I've given myself permission to be who I am. I didn't expect to move back to Finland and walk into a job as a sports coach or something in physical sciences, though that's what I'm trained to do. But I'm certainly not going to work in the gutters for ten years just so I can humbly earn the right to become a Finn. To hell with *that*.'

I noticed my voice had hardened. I was becoming agitated.

'It made me laugh out loud when I read that the greatest gap in living standards is apparently along the border between Mexico and California. Bullshit. The biggest gap in living standards is right here in Värtsilä, when you drive across the border into Ruskeala. That's when you see the begging, the filth, the dirty clothes and the tuberculosis.

Veterans with one leg sitting in the square selling their unused left shoes. That is the God's-honest truth, and in quietly accepting that truth you and all the other rich Finns are just as much the crooks as I am.'

Marja sat in silence and stared at the strip of asphalt disappearing behind us in the side mirror. I couldn't see her expression.

'Sorry for the sermon,' I said, 'but this is important... it's too big for me. Where do people's morals start and end? Where do people stop demanding we do the right thing? I don't kill people, I don't assault them or rob them, but if someone asks me to take part in a little operation whereby the government or a filthy-rich tycoon somewhere ends up earning a fraction less than they should, and I can make a living from that, then I'm in. And I sleep perfectly well at night. End of story.'

I switched off the Volvo's radio. A reporter was interviewing a Finnish expert about the drought in East Africa, the famine and various aid programmes, but I didn't want any background noise.

'That was perfect listening for this topic,' Marja said – a sign she might be relenting. 'Let's put it this way,' she added. 'I understand everything you've said and I see the logic, but I don't approve of it. I don't want to judge it because, like you said, the topic is too big. How far can we apply rules of fairness and justice? But two wrongs don't make a right, that's what I'm trying to hold onto here.'

We drove on for another few kilometres without speaking.

'Okay, I trust you,' I said. 'So, if that was a first-class truth, here's a second-class one: there might very well be skilful monks in Valamo capable of making real, beautiful old icons, and there might be some second-rate artists at the flea markets who are at their best copying the works of the great masters. You never know.'

Marja was quiet for a moment, and looked at me in the mirror.

'That sounds fair enough, so spare me the third-class truth. I appreciate you telling me all this.'

We smiled at each other in the mirror.

21

I drove to Asikkala and consulted the map to find the Larssons' summer cottage. Aarne Larsson had already told me it wasn't in any condition to be used all year round. His ex-wife Helena had told me they still had joint ownership of the cottage, and that in the summer they used it on alternate weeks.

The roads became narrower; in some places there were still patches of glinting ice on the asphalt, and I amused myself by making the Volvo slide across them. Marja wasn't impressed.

I stopped at a local farmhouse to establish the details of the final stretch of the journey. The farmer stopped mending his tractor, ushered me to the corner of his barn and showed me a few bends in the road as well as the peninsula behind which the Larssons' cottage could be found. He didn't ask why we were looking for the cottage and I didn't offer an explanation, but left him trying to make sense of the hydraulics in his Massey Ferguson.

The final section of the track leading up to the cottage hadn't been ploughed. We both commented on how differently the spring arrives: in Helsinki you could see that the grass was on the cusp of turning green again. We trudged through the ankle-high snow. The cottage was situated on the sunny side of a hill where there were some patches of bare ground; we could hear the birds singing at the arrival of spring.

Marja and I sat on the jetty, closed our eyes and let the sun warm our cheeks. We chatted about this and that.

It occurred to me that this trip would tell me much about how a relationship with Marja might pan out. Either she would accept my line of work, or she wouldn't. I'd laid things out for her, but I didn't want to make them sound rosier than they were or to keep anything hidden.

Sirje Larsson popped into my mind like another lover, anxiety spreading across my chest. There was no sign of life at the cottage, not even the marks of a skier in the snow or a fisherman's hole in the ice. Sirje was nowhere to be found here. I could scratch out another item on my list of possible leads.

It was a shame that, after this, I had no other leads to pursue.

We were knocking the loose snow from our shoes when my phone rang. The screen read simply: UNKNOWN CALLER. I asked Marja to wait in the car and walked behind the Volvo, sat on the fender and answered the call.

'It's your Uncle Olavi.' The voice was familiar, though it sounded like it was echoing and booming across a vast distance. 'Your mother told me you've got a problem and you need my help. Nice of you to remember your old relatives, though it's probably been ten years at least, eh, Viktor?'

'Well, I haven't sent any Christmas cards, that's for sure. But I'm in a spot of bother and thought I'd ask your advice. Is this line secure?'

I heard my own voice echoing a split-second late and imagined it turning into bits, then hurtling via satellites, copper leads and fibre-optic cables.

'The line's secure. At least it is for me. Otherwise I wouldn't be talking to you at all. So, tell your old uncle what's up.'

I should have called him 'Oleg', because Olavi Mylläri was really Oleg Melnikov – and had been his entire life. What's more, he wasn't my uncle but my mother's cousin, but since I was a child I'd known him as 'Uncle Olavi'.

Olavi was born in Olonets. His father Veikko had walked across the border at the end of the 1920s, served the Red Army in the Karelia Brigade and advanced to the rank of officer before being sent to the Vorkuta mines during one of Stalin's purges. It was the war that eventually saved Veikko: a Finnish-speaking officer was ideal for reconnaissance missions to Finland. Veikko died when I was a little boy, but I'd heard a lot about his spying expeditions.

I have a vivid recollection of one summer day when Olavi was visiting us with his father. They arrived on a motorbike, and Olavi warned me not to touch it. It was a large Dnepr Ural with a flat engine. They told me it was brand new. I was afraid I might burn my fingers on it, and kept a distance from the black bike.

I remembered the baking heat of that day, and the smell of the parched lawn. I tugged at Uncle Olavi's leg and asked why he was only wearing a suit and not a uniform like his father. Olavi said he was a special kind of soldier. He showed me a little red booklet decorated with patterns of wreaths, a hammer and sickle in the middle and some text on the front.

When I learned to read, I drew myself an identification card just like this. I coloured the patterns with charcoal, and with my father's ballpoint pen I carefully copied out the words *Komitet gosudarstvennoy bezopasnosti* and beneath it the letters 'KGB'. Father smiled at my card, but Mother turned serious and said some things weren't to be played with.

I calculated that Olavi – Oleg – would now be in his sixties. I told him briefly about Arkady and the services he'd asked for. Olavi listened without interrupting. By the time I'd finished, I wondered whether the line had gone dead: Olavi remained quiet.

'Well, well,' he eventually muttered. 'I thought I'd taken your name off the list, hidden you away. I don't know this "Arkady", but I imagine he's one of the new men at the embassy in Helsinki and that he's taken your name directly from the archives of his predecessors, without checking things with Moscow first.'

Again, the line fell silent for a while.

'Very well,' Olavi said at last. 'This is what's going to happen: in a few weeks I'll have a message delivered to Arkady that you're a compromised agent, but insignificant enough that we'll leave you alone. Your file will be sent to us. There will be a clerical error, perhaps, and you'll disappear for good, filed somewhere in between the letters. And I'll move Arkady to other business. But you still have to look after the Fatherland. The Mikkeli gig is something you'll have to do.'

'I don't think I have a Fatherland. But that sounds reasonable – excellent, even,' I said. 'I'm grateful, you know that. I hope this doesn't put you in any danger.'

'I'm doing this for your mother. Her heart won't hold out if you get into trouble. Besides, I'm going to retire from this business pretty soon. I've been getting things ready to leave. Looks like I might go and work for Neste Oil as a security consultant in St Petersburg.' I thought I caught a note of nostalgia in his voice. 'Right, I'm going to hang up now. Take care of the microfilms, and I'll deal with everything at this end. Don't contact me. If you have any problems, ask your mother to get word to me. All the best, Viktor.'

22

That evening I drove to Larsson's place, but once again the house looked dark. I staked out the empty street for half an hour before deciding to go to bed.

The following morning I visited Larsson's shop. I rattled the door, but it was firmly locked. He hadn't given much thought to the appearance of the shop windows. There were a few books on display – a selection of the most harmless stuff, if I gathered correctly. Maps of troop movements across the Karelian isthmus, a framed copy of Mannerheim's famous dispatch. The interior of the shop was dark. I cupped my hands around my eyes and peered inside, but the only sign of life I could see were the flashing turquoise numbers on the cash register.

I went to the doorway and rang the bells in sequence until someone trusting enough decided to buzz me into the stairwell. I walked around to the shop's rear door, crouched down and peered through the letterbox. A copy of the *Business Times* and two brown envelopes lay on the floor. I sniffed the air inside the shop, but all I could identify was the dusty smell of old books, along with a hint of tobacco smoke and the acrid smell of citrus floor detergent.

I let the letterbox clatter shut, stood up and turned to find myself staring right into the reproachful eyes of an elderly woman. I didn't stick around to explain what I was doing staring through Larsson's letterbox, and made for the door. As I pulled it shut behind me, I heard her muttering something in Swedish.

Again I visited the house in Pakila, but it looked empty. Nobody came to the door. I called Larsson's home and mobile phones, but nobody picked up. The call to his mobile was redirected to the answering machine: 'This is Aarne Larsson. I can't answer the phone right now. Please leave a message.' My investigation seemed to be going as badly as possible: first I couldn't find a trace of the person I was looking for, and now I'd lost track of my client, too.

That evening I was back at my regular stakeout. By this point, I didn't care about being seen or using an identifiable car. If anything, I hoped somebody would recognize me and come and give me some new information. Instead, I was left in peace to sit in the darkness.

I walked around the house a few times. As evening drew in, I became convinced that there was a light on inside the house, in the basement. It was just a small glimmer coming from behind the thick curtains in Larsson's office, and, on the other side, from the large windows in the living room. Perhaps the office door had been left open.

I rang the neighbour's doorbell. Marjatta Nyqvist answered. She looked as though she was about to take the dog for a walk. You have to take them out every day, I thought to myself, and wondered what else Marjatta got up to. Every time I visited, she seemed to be in exactly the same state.

'Well, hello… investigator. I've just got back from work, and was about to go out for a run with Julius.'

She invited me inside, and I sat down on the familiar sofa. Marjatta leaned coyly against the armrest of a chair. I imagined she probably had a husband who dressed in clothes that were far too young for him, who stood in front of the mirror flexing his loose stomach muscles, who played golf – and who was constantly worried his wife would cheat on him. What's more, his wife knew he was worried, and flirted with other men just enough to keep him on his toes. I hadn't quite managed to develop this scenario about their relationship all the way to her husband's impending heart attack when Marjatta spoke.

'A funny thing happened. I was talking to Aarne Larsson the other day, and I mentioned that the investigator looking into Sirje's disappearance had popped in and talked to me. I thought I'd best be upfront with him. He was very matter-of-fact, but if I'm not wrong, he referred to you by a different name. The card you gave me said your name was "Kesonen".'

Marjatta gave me that feminine smile of hers, and I caught a sweet whiff of her perfume.

'I thought it might make a more trustworthy first impression than "V. Kärppä",' I said, trying to sound cheerful in telling her the truth while looking at her with the utmost seriousness. 'I'm sorry for misleading you.'

'I was expecting you to come back sooner or later. Would you like a coffee or something?' Marjatta prolonged forgiving me with the languid ease of a woman in her forties.

'Thank you, but I don't think I'll have time.' I tried to focus on the photograph of Sirje Larsson and her husband's abrasive accusation that a Russian was always a good-for-nothing – though I could easily have thought of something else Marjatta might have offered me. 'I've been trying to get hold of Aarne Larsson for a few days now, but haven't been able to find him. His shop is shut, and there's no sign in the window to say why. You'd think he would keep his clients informed if he'd gone off on a trip somewhere...'

'Somewhere like a collectible book festival in Johannesburg!' she laughed. 'I know my neighbour well enough that I know the kind of things he gets up to. Well, it doesn't bother me. I haven't seen him for goodness knows how long, but I've been working evenings a lot. So I don't know whether he's away on business, or what he's doing.'

I hauled myself up from this lovely woman's sofa, said goodbye, walked around Larsson's house one more time and returned to my Volvo. I felt queasy. I knew I'd have to get inside Larsson's house one way or another, and I didn't like the thought one bit. I was afraid of going into the house, but more than that I was afraid of giving in to my fears.

I had to get inside. But first I called my mother. She sounded cheerful, and started telling me enthusiastically about the migratory birds and how much work Karpov's helpers had been doing.

'I know they're crooks,' she said. 'But they're polite to an old woman like me... And what do you know? That Arkady Makarov, the one who used to drive Valery about, well, he's Svetlana Mihailyevna's boy. His mother used to milk the cows when I was an accountant at the *sovkhoz* in Helylä.'

At least in Sortavala, everything seemed to be business as usual.

I waited in the car until nearly midnight. I figured it was wiser to keep the car in one place than to drive back and forth. If anyone started looking for a burglar, the Volvo had already been seen many times. Perhaps it was better that it had been parked on the street in full view all evening.

I'd taken my helpful bag of tricks out of the boot in good time. I couldn't remember seeing evidence of an alarm system on the doors and windows. The easiest way to get into the house would be through the garage. I picked out a suitable set of tools: I'm not a locksmith, but I know how to pick standard Abloy and Boda locks. And if necessary, I could always open the window with a diamond cutter.

I sneaked up to the garage door, pulled on a thin pair of gloves and managed to prise the lock open in ten minutes. The Saab was still there. The garage smelled like a clean, dry cellar – no traces of motor grease or oil. Larsson didn't seem like a do-it-yourself kind of man. I wanted to go from the garage into the house through the boiler room, but a large steel door stood in my way. The door had no padlock or keyhole; it was locked from the inside with what must have been a sturdy bolt.

I walked carefully back into the yard, pulled back the garage door, locked it again and made my way back around to the entrance to the guest room. I played around with the lock for a long time, and was about to give up when I finally managed to get its teeth to move inwards. I'd left a scratch on the doorframe; a professional would have been ashamed.

I opened the door just enough to slip into the porch. A chair stood in front of the inner door but it slid out of the way, letting me into what was once the servant's room. It still looked ready to accommodate non-existent guests.

I tried to walk evenly, using the full rubber soles of my shoes to make my steps as silent as possible. If I hadn't been so nervous, I would probably have laughed at such caution.

After all, I'd been watching the house for days without seeing a living soul.

But it wasn't the living I was afraid of. It was the dead.

At home, I'd always been told the human body is nothing but matter. My grandparents had died before my birth and my father was buried without much ceremony. Still, I'd been to many Orthodox funerals with an open casket, where the bereaved paid their final respects to the deceased, touched the body and even kissed it.

Dead people freaked me out.

I'd sat in saunas, drunk vodka, worked and played sports with murderers. Their arms were covered in prison tattoos, emblems of their bloody work, but none of that bothered me. It was harmless corpses that frightened me, not the harmful people who made them.

Death hung in the air inside Larsson's house. Perhaps it was a smell – like the smell nestling beneath the sweet scent of flowers at funerals – or nothing more than an inkling. Animals can sense death, and I don't believe our ability to sense danger can have disappeared altogether after only a few generations of living in warm houses.

I walked cautiously around the lower floor of Larsson's house, lighting my way with a small metallic flashlight. The kitchen was as empty and clinical as an operating theatre. The living room seemed to have been left in the same state in which I'd seen it when I'd last visited the house. The office door was ajar, and a faint light emanated from inside. I pushed the door open slowly. The floor lamp next to Larsson's reading chair was switched on, shining a warm light some ways into the room and spreading the smell of burned specks of dust through the air. The room was silent. Not even the clock on the desk was ticking. Perhaps its batteries were dead. After batteries die, the machinery can continue working for a day or so. That could tell us something, I told myself, using rational thinking to try to keep my growing sense of dread at bay.

The upper floor was empty. 'Like Jesus's tomb after Easter,' I said out loud. That was something Korhonen had once said, and I regretted the profanity at once. *Gospodi,* I whispered, and wondered which way you were supposed to make the sign of the cross: right or left first.

I took a deep breath and peered through the gap in the curtains out into the yard, but there was nobody there. Then I walked down into the basement. I remembered there weren't any windows in the hobby room, so I switched on the lights. Aarne Larsson looked me right in the eyes.

Perhaps it would be more appropriate to say he seemed to be looking at me. His eyes didn't follow me, and his eyelids didn't blink as I jumped to one side. From now on, all Larsson would watch were channels from the other side: he was dead.

His body was sitting upright in a chair a metre away from the desk. I walked cautiously around it. A length of metal wire was sunk into his throat. It had been pulled behind his back and tied in a quick knot, the ends of the wire neatly wound around the levers adjusting the back of the chair.

Larsson's hands rested on his thighs. The expression on his face was one of surprise, and his skin was a mottled shade of red and violet. He looked about as alive as a Polaroid passport photograph. He wore a dark-grey pair of trousers and the cardigan I'd seen before with the leather patches. His reading glasses had fallen to the floor; they must have been in his hands when he'd died. The slippers looked inappropriate, offensively worthless in the face of death. Larsson should have been killed outdoors, or at the very least in a pair of decent leather brogues instead of these threadbare house shoes.

I examined the room, though I had the sense I was looking in vain. The people who killed Larsson were professionals. On the desk was a book in the press, ready to be bound. *The Churches of Ceded Karelia* was to be Larsson's last work.

23

Once back in the car, I took off my gloves and called Korhonen. His mobile phone rang for a long time, and eventually I was put through to the answering machine. I pressed the red button, then the green immediately afterwards. The screen of my Nokia informed me I was CALLING KORHONEN.

This time, he answered. He sounded like he'd just woken up.

'Hosni Mubarak speaking. This had better be important, Kärppä.'

'It is,' I said. 'So important that I didn't fancy leaving a message after the beep. Is that the kind of English they teach you at the police academy? Get in the car and drive down to the Larssons' house. Larsson is in there, dead. The old man, that is.'

Korhonen thought about this quietly for a minute, then spoke, his voice now somewhat livelier. 'Tell me what happened. I want to hear everything. The truth.'

I explained that I'd drawn a blank on the Sirje Larsson case. I needed more information about her and her relationship with Aarne, and when he disappeared too, I had to break into the house.

'I went in tidily and came out even more tidily,' I said. 'Keep me out of this, okay?'

'You didn't knock the wind out of him yourself, did you? Or maybe Sirje Larsson is set to inherit everything from the old guy, and you decided to help her out. I suppose you're shagging her on the side,' Korhonen scoffed. 'We should start calling you the Ladoga Lothario.'

'For Christ's sake, of course I'm not shagging her. It's exactly as I said. Besides, he didn't have the wind knocked out of him. More like the wind stopped flowing altogether. He was strangled with metal wire. It was a professional job. But it wasn't me. I'm an amateur when it comes to this kind of stuff. I'm guessing Lillepuu took out a contract on his brother-in-law.' I told him about Lillepuu's insinuations, and the fact that he'd been watching Larsson's house too.

'I don't care whether you're an amateur or a *souteneur*. Let's assume I believe some of what you've told me,' Korhonen continued. 'I might keep you out of it, but you'll owe me quite a few favours.'

'Oh, really? If you ask me, our accounts are tipped the other way. I've just brought you a fresh corpse and a suspect. It would have been far more unpleasant to go into that house if Larsson had been left to mature in there for a few weeks.'

I downed a manly amount of vodka before falling into bed and sleeping like a baby. I had a series of restless dreams: Aarne Larsson playing golf; Sirje appearing on the house steps calling people in for coffee, a small pot in her hand; Mother and Marja sitting at the coffee table, a smart white tablecloth, a round cake, slices cut and served. *'Goodness, this is the least you should have at a funeral,' says Mother.*

I couldn't really grasp the fragments of my dreams, or perhaps they weren't meant to develop into a story. I awoke after nine, tired and sweaty, and forced myself into action, pumping up my muscles with a set of press-ups and stomach and back exercises. As I went to the shower, I saw in the mirror that my eyelids were swollen with fluid, and my face was ruddy. The colour was almost violet, like someone with high blood pressure – or like Aarne Larsson's corpse.

I called Marja, but she'd already left for the university; she kept her phone on silent when she was in the library or sitting in lectures. All I could do was wait for what happened next.

I went to my office, placed my Chinese pistol in the holster on my back and made sure my Smith & Wesson revolver was in the half-open drawer of my desk. I sat down and tried to read Stephen Hawking's *A Brief History of Time*, which I'd picked up at the second-hand shop round the corner. I imagined I understood long sections of the book, though my concentration came in fits and starts. All the while I kept an eye out for movement across the square and on the street. I had more reason to expect Estonian guests than Larsson had.

I finished reading Hawking and began a new book titled *Born from Emptiness*, a Finnish theoretical physicist's analysis of the structure of the universe. My mobile beeped and I clicked open the text message. It was from Karpov. 'Cigarettes and stewing steak paid in full. Same price.'

Normally, I would have at least sniggered at Valery's cryptic language, but this time I wanted to be sure. I locked the office, walked around the square, bought another phone card at the kiosk and called Karpov from a phone box.

'So you've been taking care of our southern neighbour?' I got straight to the point without introducing myself.

'That's right,' he replied jovially.

'Where can I find him? Or is he in many places all at once? It would be a damn fine thing if we could pin him down. Now.'

'He's fetching spare parts for his BMW,' Karpov replied quickly.

'Okay, got it,' I said.

I hung up, walked back across the square and dialled Korhonen's number.

'Lauttasaari Port and Starboard, Korhonen speaking,' the policeman snapped.

'It's Kärppä.'

Korhonen interrupted me before I could say anything else: 'Now, now, no need to rush. Jesus is coming, didn't you hear? He's been spotted on the outskirts of town. Listen, Kärppä, I'm having lunch. Is this important?'

'Not really. But I thought you might be interested to know that Lillepuu can be found in the car park outside Biltema in a black or dark-blue BMW. He's waiting there, and won't be going anywhere any time soon.' I continued, determined not to let Korhonen get a word in: 'I haven't taken care of him, either, but you'll remember the matter of the stolen cigarettes. There were plenty of people who wanted to put Jaak out of business.'

Korhonen said he'd call the coroner's office and go for a little drive, then added that he hoped I didn't have all that many more bodies lined up for him. 'Though this is one way to keep criminals off the streets,' he sighed.

Ryshkov was waiting outside my office, in his Mercedes. He followed me inside, his expression serious, and lit a cigarette.

'I've just got out of the station, spent all morning being grilled by the police,' he sighed. 'Your friend Korhonen hauled me out of bed. I was still asleep. He held me up against the wall and accused me of killing Aarne Larsson. I didn't even know him – or his wife. Do I have you to thank for this? Is it you that's got me caught up in this mess?'

'Absolutely not. I told Korhonen it was the Estonians who killed Larsson. He probably thinks I'm telling him a pack of lies, that it was me that took care of Larsson, probably with a bit of help from you. Either that, or he wants to look like he's investigating the case, though he knows perfectly well who was behind it. Well, he won't be able to convict Lillepuu now. There wasn't much evidence to start with, and to make matters worse I just got word that Lillepuu has been taken out, too. Korhonen is on his way to pick up the body in the car park outside Biltema,' I explained.

I was surprised to see Ryshkov smiling, giving me a glimpse of his golden incisor. 'I know that,' he said. 'That's why I was so surprised at Korhonen's cross-examination. We paid Lillepuu a little visit last night. Me, one of Karpov's men and one of my boys. The three of us.'

I couldn't say a word, not even to admire his quick action and efficiency.

'Nice place he's got in the West End,' Ryshkov continued. 'It's a surprisingly quick journey into town; the traffic along Länsiväylä moves pretty fast. It's a nice apartment, but the security system isn't up to much, for a man in his position.' Then Ryshkov said, matter-of-factly, 'We shot him.'

He continued: 'We took the body down to the highway in his own BMW. Still, it's not his car any longer, is it? You know what I mean. We popped into the store to get a set of windscreen wipers and decorated hubcaps and drove away in a different car. We thought someone was bound to recognize the car before long, and find the body. And the news of Lillepuu's death will get around pretty quick. You'll find plenty of Russians and Estonians hanging around that car park right now.'

24

The town was buzzing for a few days after the murders of Larsson and Lillepuu. The tabloids attempted to link the two cases, but Korhonen tried to get out a theory about a struggle between a gang of hardened Estonian criminals in which Aarne Larsson, innocent bystander and patriot, got caught up.

For a while, the headlines also delighted in the missing 'Estonian beauty'. Sirje Larsson's now-familiar, shy expression stared at me in the grainy advertisements at newspaper kiosks. To my relief, I'd managed to keep myself out of the headlines. Life was made calmer by the fact that an eyewitness claimed to have seen the men suspected of killing Larsson. A man standing on his balcony having a cigarette in the house opposite was convinced he had seen Lillepuu going into Larsson's house, accompanied by a young man.

Korhonen came to my office, asking about the case. I explained that Lillepuu's killers were Russian, and that they wouldn't be in the country any longer. 'It was a clean kill. Just the way you wanted.'

'I suppose you're right,' said Korhonen, muttering to himself and pacing up and down my office. Parjanne was sitting in the car, like a glum dog left in the car park outside a shopping mall, with the window rolled down an inch.

'But there's something not quite right about this. They all seem to have died too conveniently. The bad guys kill each other like kids playing tag. I don't think I can stitch you up for this, but Sirje keeps bugging me,' Korhonen puffed, and turned on the old linoleum floor.

'I've been confused all along,' I tried to assure him. 'Aarne Larsson hired me to find his wife, but I couldn't come up with anything. Lillepuu hinted that Larsson knew far more than he was letting on. Did Larsson kill his own wife and then pretend to look for her by hiring me, a gullible Russian? If that's the case, he knew perfectly well I'd draw a blank. But why would he kill his wife? Sure, he was a bit eccentric, but that doesn't make him a murderer.'

Korhonen stepped to the window... the filing cabinet... the window...

'That's what I thought, too,' he said. 'Larsson was disappointed in his wife. She might have had some kind of romantic encounter, or she simply wasn't the paragon of purity he'd imagined. Perhaps Larsson expected someone a bit smarter. Though a woman's stupidity never normally gets in the way of things... You know the difference between a wife and a dog? You can't tease a dog over the phone,' Korhonen said philosophically, his expression remaining concerned and decorous throughout. 'At first, I looked for signs of an affair, but couldn't find any. I suppose you didn't fare much better?'

I shook my head. 'But a few people said Larsson had a quick temper, he'd call his wife a "stupid tart" – stress on the word *stupid* – a "Russian hooker", that kind of thing,' I continued. 'Perhaps Sirje Larsson supported Tarja Halonen for President. From what I know of Larsson, that alone would have been enough to warrant the death penalty.'

'Until a body turns up, we can't be sure,' Korhonen muttered. 'But if Sirje is alive, she'll put in an appearance sooner or later.'

'I think Sirje is already dead,' I said. 'Perhaps hiring me was a bluff. Either that, or Larsson wanted me to find Sirje and find him out. Lillepuu decided to carry out his own sentence first.'

Marja was studying for final exams, but we managed to meet up, go to the cinema and have a beer – though I don't much care for beer. I started going for long runs with Marja riding her bike alongside me.

'You're a funny guy, you know that?' Marja said. 'It's hard to say what you are.' She was sitting on my bed, leaning against the headboard and hugging her knees beneath the duvet.

'Oh,' I said, and lay quietly on my stomach, a pillow beneath my neck, my eyes closed. 'Is that the Professor's professional opinion?'

'Your actions always seem to depend on your surroundings; you behave the way you think people want you to behave. Or it's as though you're playing a role, making sure people think of you what you want them to think.' Her tone was earnest.

I thought about this for a moment. 'But doesn't everybody do that? We are always defined by other people. It works both ways.'

'Of course,' said Marja. 'I don't mean normal communication, which is instinctive and very deeply ingrained within us. Humans give each other signals about themselves and their intentions, just as a dog wags its tail. But you do this twice over: you wonder whether or not you should wag your tail at all, and you think carefully about what other people will think about the tail-wagging… about you.'

I rolled on my side and stared at the wall. I recalled that, as a child, I would stare at the twists and turns of the varnished wooden panels on the ceiling and imagine they represented all different kinds of animals. We slept on a pullout wooden sofa in the living room. Alexei always fell asleep first, snoring and talking in his sleep; I would be tucked in safely against the wall and lie there awake, thinking about things for hours, though I was the younger of us two brothers. I knew Marja would have liked this story, but I decided not to tell her.

Marja tousled my hair. 'Don't worry. The real Viktor shines through, all right. You might think you can, but you can't control everything. And the hidden Viktor is the most fascinating of all. You can relax and be yourself, let go, trust other people, trust yourself. You're just fine the way you are.'

Marja twisted a curl of my hair around her finger. I kept my eyes closed and tried to lie there calmly, listening as she told a story.

'Humphrey Bogart was at a party once. Somebody came up and teased him, saying, "You're not really a tough guy, you just play tough roles." Bogart didn't say anything, just bit off a piece of his whiskey glass and ate it – and probably the rest of the glass too.'

She paused. 'I think it was a bit unnecessary, a bit over the top, but it probably had the desired effect on the women present. He wanted to look like an alpha male. What's interesting is how soft and gentle Bogart could appear, too.'

'There was an Uzbek guy in the army with me who ate pieces of glass if we paid him. We'd have a whip-round for a few dozen roubles. I don't think he was right in the head. Who is Humphrey Bogart?' I asked innocently.

Marja looked at me in disbelief, hit me with a pillow and called me a charlatan as she started to laugh.

25

I was somewhat taken aback when Helena Larsson walked into my office.

'I'm sorting out Aarne's affairs. He didn't have any relatives, and seeing as there's no news on Sirje's whereabouts... It won't be a big funeral, just a simple blessing and cremation here in Helsinki. That's what Kimmo wanted. He is Aarne's son, after all.'

My client's ex-wife stood there for a moment, looking pensive and biting her lip. 'I wanted to ask you if there's any news about Sirje's disappearance, and whether or not you still have some lines of investigation outstanding. Among Aarne's bills is a note to pay you ten thousand marks with the reference "S. Larsson Case. Final Payment." Don't worry, I've paid this from his estate. But I wondered whether the payment was late, because it was dated last week.'

Helena grew silent, then said: 'It really would be nice to get some closure on this case. It sounds terrible to talk about such morbid matters at a time like this, but Kimmo is his father's heir, and we must at least find out what happened to Sirje. She will have to be declared either missing or dead. We're not talking about any great sums of money. We owned the house half-and-half. Sirje had no stake in the property.

But as for the business and the summer cottage… It's going to be quite a mess.'

I had already resigned myself to the fact that the case of Sirje Larsson would remain unsolved. She could be in Sweden happily producing oil paintings, or rotting in a ditch in Hyrylä. In my mind, I had already put the case file in a folder and slid that folder to the back of the filing cabinet.

I sighed and asked Helena Larsson to leave me the house keys. I would have to go through Aarne and Sirje Larsson's house again in detail. Aarne wanted this case solved once and for all. And he had already paid me for it.

Mother heard straight away that something was bothering me. 'Well, son, what's on your mind?' she asked, trying to coax it out of me.

I told her I didn't much like bodies, but now they'd been turning up a little too frequently. I assured her I had nothing to do with any of the killings.

'I didn't think you did; not for a second. But you must look after yourself, now. I'm not afraid of death any more. It comes to us all sooner or later.' She said this so abruptly that it startled me. 'But I don't think my time is up just yet… It's suddenly so warm here! Are you planning another visit? I know it's a long drive. The sound of the birds is so beautiful…'

I said I hoped her good health continued, ended the call, locked the office and returned to the Larssons' house.

It felt strange driving up to the front door and walking inside with my own set of keys. I rummaged about, deliberately making a noise, and moved around as I pleased, though there was nobody there to watch me. I decided to give the house a thorough going-over, to open every cupboard and look in the furthest corner of every drawer.

After two hours of work, I was only a few scraps of information wiser. The medicine cabinet had revealed the couple's general state of health. Sirje suffered from a pollen allergy; the cabinet contained a packet of antihistamine tablets and a bottle of eye drops. Judging by the best-before labels, both had been purchased the previous spring. Aarne Larsson was on medication to keep his blood pressure down, but apart from that the couple got by with nothing stronger than painkillers. There was no sign of contraceptive pills. In the nightstand on Aarne's side of the bed was an opened packet of Sultan condoms. I smirked. I hadn't imagined Larsson to be the kind of man to arouse his partner with anything involving different flavours.

The drinks cabinet contained a selection of whiskies, bottles of cognac and vodka, all now gathering dust. Most of the bottles were unopened. It seemed the Larssons lived a fairly sober, healthy life and didn't need chemicals to spice things up.

I sat in Aarne's reading chair, placed defiantly beneath the model airplane with the swastika, for a long time. I flicked through his books and company files. Larsson's second-hand book business had profits of about a million marks a year. He sold books, translated and published works by European thinkers I had never heard of in a series titled *Free-Thinking Books,* and paid himself a monthly salary of 15,000 marks. Everything about the business seemed open, transparent and above board.

Larsson had also kept meticulous records of his home finances. He paid his ex-wife rent for his share of the house, but apart from that the family's outgoings were surprisingly small. Their healthy lifestyle meant the family could survive on very little indeed. The receipts didn't give a miserly impression, either: food and clothes were generally bought from Stockmann's department store; the couple had also travelled to the Mediterranean, spent time in the capitals of Europe and regularly went to a restaurant for Sunday lunch. The Larssons' lifestyle was simply one that didn't involve much money.

I lay back on Larsson's bed and stared at the ceiling, trying to imagine what Sirje Larsson had been thinking when she went to sleep each night. I pictured Aarne standing by the bed in his pyjamas, winding the old-fashioned alarm clock, checking the time and climbing in next to her. What had they talked about? How had Sirje discussed her desires – or did she have any at all? I lifted the bedspread, pressed the pillow against my face and imagined I caught Sirje's faint scent.

I sat down by the television and went through the row of videos. Most of the cassettes contained exactly what was written on the spine: a documentary about the Berlin Airlift, *Die Hard 2*, *The Dirty Dozen*. The Larssons hadn't put together their own archive of family footage, and it seemed there was no pornography hidden behind the labels.

Likewise, the kitchen cupboards provided more evidence of a simple, healthy life. Oat flakes, but no exotic spices; an expensive-looking set of frying pans, but no wok; rapeseed oil, but no black olives.

I turned on the tap and waited for the water to cool to drinking temperature. I thought about the house; I would have to go through the basement one more time, then I would have searched the house from top to bottom, from the attic to its foundations. Surely there must be a loft or attic space above the house, I thought. The realization startled me. I dashed up the stairs. The ceilings on the upper floor had been panelled over, and there didn't seem to be any way into the loft.

In the walk-in closet I pulled the hangers with Sirje's blouses and trousers to one side, stood on a chair and lifted the storage boxes from the upper shelf. Bingo! In the ceiling was a hatch on a set of hinges, locked shut with two bolts.

I fetched a stepladder from the kitchen and opened the hatch, which was surprisingly thick with layers of insulation. I climbed up, and once on the top step I had to balance on tiptoe in order to reach into the loft and haul myself up on my elbows. The cool air smelled of wood and sawdust. My head was damp with sweat.

The attic was dark. I grimaced and balanced on the stepladder as I fumbled in my pocket for my torch. I aimed the narrow beam of light across each section of the space. The house had been built in the 1930s, but had been renovated recently. The upper floor was covered in sawdust, on top of which a layer of glass-fibre insulation had been placed. The rafters were made of thick, old wood and the beams across the floor looked original.

I grimaced again. What exactly had I been expecting to find up here? The hatch into the attic was so small, and in such an awkward place, that Sirje would have needed a full ladder to get up there. The body could hardly have been dragged up into the attic – at least, Aarne Larsson wouldn't have been able to do it by himself. I closed the hatch carefully and straightened the clothes hanging in the closet.

The Churches of Ceded Karelia was still in the book press in the cellar, awaiting its leather cover. Like everything in the house, Larsson's tools were all kept in neat order. Even old newspapers had been bound together with string into tight bundles, ready to be taken to the recycling bin.

The boiler room contained nothing but the green oil-heated boiler and two pairs of rubber boots side by side, the larger pair black and the smaller pair red. The modern-looking plastic oil container had been placed in the cellar. The garage was as tidy as it had been the last time I visited. Propped by the front door stood a snow shovel and a broom. A set of summer tires hung on hooks in the wall, but apart from that the garage walls were empty. The Saab was unlocked. I sat down in the driver's seat as though I were inspecting it on Ruuskanen's forecourt. The car smelled new, though it had 44,359 kilometres on the odometer. In my mind's eye I could see the ad in the newspaper: PERFECT INSPECTION RECORD, VEHICLE INHERITED THROUGH A WILL.

The glove compartment contained the car's registration papers, mechanics' bills, a pair of sunglasses and a tin of hard-boiled fruit caramels. I took a lemon-smelling sweet, but it began to taste sour when I realized I was eating a dead man's throat pastilles. I opened the boot, which contained an aluminium snow shovel, a green tarpaulin, a tool set and an electric chainsaw.

I sat down in the chair at Larsson's desk, though I remembered his glassy eyes only too well as he had sat there, his face red and blue, a length of steel wire embedded in his throat.

Aarne Larsson had known what was happening; he'd had time to see and recognize his killer. Perhaps they had even spoken, and Jaak Lillepuu had pronounced his death sentence. I imagined that Larsson probably hadn't begged for mercy. He hadn't put up a fight as Lillepuu's henchman stepped behind the chair, twisted the metal wire into a noose round Larsson's neck and pulled it tight. Larsson and Lillepuu had looked each other in the eye, Jaak watching as the light in his brother-in-law's eyes slowly diminished.

My imagination chilled the basement so much that I found myself shivering. I got up from the chair, walked past the shelves on the walls, leaned against the freezer and read through the spines of the books and folders on the shelves for the third time. A piece of paper had been taped to the freezer door, listing its contents: 'Strawberries (500g), 15 July', and beside this a series of lines that I guessed must have denoted the number of tubs. Some of the lines had been crossed out, but I could see that there were several kilos of strawberries left. The list also detailed elk meat, fish and bread, though I guessed that in this house, the freezer would remain in good order even without an inventory of its contents.

I opened the lid. A small light flickered on, and I was taken aback at the sheer volume of frozen goods. I lifted tubs of strawberries and bags of bread to one side. Beneath them were frozen vegetable packs, and underneath the frost I could make out frozen meat in plastic freezer bags. I turned them; at the bottom of the freezer were plastic carrier bags containing larger pieces of animal carcass.

There was no mention on the contents list of any racks of lamb left over from Easter, I thought, and the elk appeared to be in smaller parcels. I pulled off the tape and prised one of the bags open. My fingers touched something soft. I had just enough time to wonder why this hadn't frozen like everything else when I felt and saw the black hairs in my fingers. I forced myself to look one more time, slammed the freezer door shut and vomited on the hobby-room rug.

I had found Sirje.

26

I spent the night at Marja's place. We didn't really argue, but we nagged at and complained to each other. In the morning, I drank my tea and told her I'd be going to Mikkeli for the day. Marja poured yoghurt over her muesli and stood in her short nightdress with her back to me. I could see her panties beneath the hem of her skirt when she leaned against the counter and rested one foot on top of the other.

Marja didn't ask to join me, and I didn't ask about her plans. She didn't like me asking too many questions. 'This is the way I am, and you'll just have to trust me and accept me,' she always said in a tone that meant this was the end of the discussion. She reminded me that, with my past, there was no point expecting to meet the Virgin Mary.

Even I began to wonder why it was that a strange job offer didn't seem to faze me at all, but the proximity of a woman always made me restless. You can't control everything, I told myself, repeating what Marja had said. I realized that, while the success of the Mikkeli job was up to me, I couldn't change Marja one way or the other.

Korhonen was waiting for me in front of my office. He left Parjanne in the car and walked inside after me, propped himself in the doorway and flicked cigarette ash on the floor.

'You're a big man, but nobody ever taught you about cleanliness. Don't you care about personal hygiene?' I asked, and tapped the ashtray. 'You're up early,' I added.

'You haven't brought me any new bodies for a while,' Korhonen quipped. 'Several days in a row without a fresh corpse. I'll have withdrawal symptoms before long.'

'Don't remind me. I'm a sensitive man. Thinking about Sirje doesn't exactly make me feel great.'

'Sensitive as an old woman, you. I thought you'd like to know the lab confirmed that the body parts in the freezer definitely belonged to Sirje Larsson. The DNA was a match. They found dental records for her in Estonia and took samples during Jaak's post-mortem. They were brother and sister, all right. Their old father had to identify her, from the head. Hard to say which of their smiles was stiffer.' Korhonen chortled, though I could see a bead of sweat on his forehead; his cigarette trembled in his fingers.

'How was she killed?' I asked. I had to force myself to listen as Korhonen explained.

'Smothered, probably with a pillow over the face. The fibre samples weren't conclusive. Then the body was cut up using the electric saw, right there in the garage. Larsson probably let her bleed out, washed the blood down the drain, then picked up the Black & Decker and got to work.' Korhonen really knew how to spin a yarn. 'Larsson cleaned the floor, the saw and tarpaulin all right, but that kind of thing always leaves a trace. It was a hell of a case.'

'What happened to Jaak's body? I mean, where was it buried?'

'Their father had just identified the body, and he'd taken the coffin with him on the ferry back to Tallinn. I was there to hand it over; there always has to be an officer present. Jaak's face was a mess, too. It can't have been nice having to identify it. The old man was trying to put on a brave face, but it must have been tough. And no sooner had he got back when he had to come and identify his daughter too, and take another coffin back to Estonia.'

Neither of us spoke for a moment, as if out of respect for the dead. I wonder how Aino Lillepuu had coped with losing two children, but thinking about this was too much. Korhonen broke the silence. He got up as though he had suddenly had enough of loitering in my office, muttered something in the doorway and left.

Ryshkov arrived five minutes later.

'What did the police want?' he asked, without bothering to greet me.

'Just wanted to tell me they've identified the body as that of Sirje Larsson.'

'Nothing else? Good.'

Ryshkov's eyes and his golden tooth flashed as he gave a quick smile. 'We've got a quick job in Tallinn. We're going to fetch some goods, bring back a few cars.'

'I've got another job on today,' I tried to protest. 'I have to go to Mikkeli.'

Ryshkov looked me in the eyes and walked up close to me, staring so intensely that I felt as though blinking would have offended him. He leaned his head to one side and pinched my cheek like a child.

'Viktor, Viktor,' he said playfully, moved his hand to my hair and gently tugged. 'When I say we've got a job in Tallinn, that means there are no other jobs. I've always liked you,

Viktor… there's something soft and nice about you. You've grown up surrounded by women. But sometimes I find I have to boss you around like a child.'

These were surprisingly long sentences for Ryshkov. He spoke softly, like a psychoanalyst on daytime television, then slowly moved his hand away and ruffled my hair. A chill ran through me. I thought of a dog whose master strokes it and talks to it in soft, consoling tones before shooting it in the back of the head.

'Take your papers with you. You won't need anything else. We'll be back on the ferry this evening.'

Ryshkov stepped towards the door. I pulled on my coat, and from the filing cabinet I took out some money and my passport. And my Chinese pistol.

The Mercedes was sitting outside my office, guzzling diesel. The driver was a man I hadn't seen before, a clone of all Ryshkov's men: 182 centimetres tall and 85 kilos in weight, give or take, with short hair, wearing a smart, dark-brown leather jacket and a pair of light trousers.

I was about to sit in the back but was surprised to find a slender young woman in a black jacket sitting there instead. She gave me a curious look with her dark eyes. The woman slid over to the middle seat, and the girl sitting on the other side gave an exaggerated 'ouch!' before saying something indistinct and uptight in Russian. She seemed to be complaining about the crush, the hurry and how stupid everything was. The girl could have been twelve, fourteen or sixteen. She was wearing dark sunglasses and had carefully styled hair, light jeans and a jacket.

'My wife will be taking the girl to school as soon as we get to the port,' Ryshkov explained, combining the introductions with the answer to a question I hadn't yet asked.

I shook the woman's hand and introduced myself in Russian. Yelena Ryshkova began chatting away while her daughter, Oksana, stuck to a mumbled formal greeting. As she spoke I caught sight of braces on her teeth, before she turned and concentrated on staring out the window and listening to music through her earphones. The faint beat of the music could be heard in the car as though an arrhythmic swarm of crickets was hidden beneath the back seat.

During the short drive to the port, we covered Yelena's family roots near St Petersburg and her daughter's academic success at the Russian school in Helsinki. She was about to finish Year 9; her language skills were good, but she also had a keen interest in mathematics and was preparing a flute recital for the school's end-of-term gala. The girl had a musical bent, which she clearly inherited from her father, though she had dropped out of ballet school.

Ryshkov gave a heavy sigh in the front seat, yet he seemed to be more interested in the morning traffic through the town. At each corner he turned his head and looked, almost synchronized with the driver. It looked as though their skulls were joined by a lever. My boss kept well out of the conversation in the back seat. He wasn't the kind of man to have a photograph of his children glued to the inside of his wallet.

At the entrance to the ferry terminal, Ryshkov and I stepped out of the car. Ryshkov bid his family a curt goodbye. I was more profuse in my farewells and wished his wife and daughter well, though Oksana still had her nose pressed tight against the window. Ryshkov took the now familiar-looking Diadora sports bag from the boot and marched towards the entrance. I followed him. The fast ferry was already sucking queues of travellers on board, and he breezed through passport control. I walked behind him like a little boy. The image would have been complete if I'd been holding on to the hem of his coat.

The ferry was full. Ryshkov found two empty seats facing each other diagonally, and slumped down in one of them. He closed his eyes and dozed off almost instantly.

I sat down and thought. I watched Ryshkov. Beneath one of his eyelids I could make out a thin sliver of his eye, white and brown, and for a moment I wondered whether or not he was watching me after all. His heavy breathing sounded genuine; at times he was almost snoring. Strange spluttering noises emanated from his throat as he cleared phlegm from his gullet. I lay back as far as I could, closed my eyes and tried to relax my muscles and my mind. The barrel of the pistol was pressing against my buttock, but adjusting the position of my firearm at this stage was out of the question.

Upon arrival at the harbour in Tallinn we were again met by a Mercedes, this time a new diplomatic car in a rich shade of black. Ryshkov went straight to the front seat; I sat in the back. The driver greeted us quietly in Russian, didn't ask any questions and set off immediately. He was a small man; in his hands, the Mercedes' steering wheel was like a ship's helm. It looked as though he had to crane his neck to see over the top of it. His hair was dark and thinning, and he had a black beard, dark eyes and golden brown skin. I guessed he must have been from somewhere in the Caucasus or Central Asia. I didn't ask.

We first headed east towards Narva, but before long the driver had taken so many turns through the labyrinthine streets of Tallinn that I was no longer sure of our direction.

We ended up in an industrial park lined with rows of steel-framed buildings, abandoned plots of land and old, low-rise warehouses.

The Mercedes wobbled into the rectangular forecourt. The gravel was dotted with small puddles, as if perforated by a giant knitting needle. The yard was surrounded by a fence that looked as if it had been welded together during the Soviet years, at the Kirov factory near Leningrad. (I remembered the echo of the Metro announcement – *Kirovski Zavoda* – as I had lived next to the enormous plant and its Metro station.) There were bars across the fences, twisted nails and a logo of the sun on the gates. The oblong building was made of grey bricks. It had many entrances: modern aluminium up-and-over doors large enough to drive a truck through, narrow blue wooden doors placed irregularly along the wall. There were only a few windows, and they were grey with dirt.

In the yard were items of furniture neatly packaged in plastic, piles of rusty pipes and rods and smooth, threadbare tires stacked up to head height. A skinny man in overalls was mending an old Scania truck. He crawled out from beneath the vehicle, stretched his stiff limbs and seemed surprised as he looked at the cardan shaft and universal joint he had just removed from the chassis beneath the truck. The man nodded in our direction, but didn't talk to us.

Ryshkov opened one of the nameless doors and stepped inside. I followed him. The corridor was surprisingly tidy. The smooth walls smelled of fresh paint, and there was frosted glass in the doors on the landings. Ryshkov opened another one of the doors. The sign on it read: AUTOTRANSBALTICA.

'There are some people you know here, though you haven't met all of them,' said Ryshkov, and gave a curious smile.

He showed me into the room with exaggerated courtesy. I had just enough time to note how clean the space was. It contained a white Volkswagen van and a small Mitsubishi flatbed, trucks stacked high with boxes of Nokia mobile phones and packing material, barrels propped along the walls and a desk to one side of the space. There were Adidas tracksuits in plastic bags, computers and office equipment.

I tried to concentrate on everything except the two people sitting behind the desk: a tall, thin man leaned against the table talking on his mobile phone, and a dark-haired woman, who was almost beautiful and at first glance resembled the man, sat calmly in a chair, swinging back and forth. Jaak and Sirje Lillepuu looked alive and surprisingly well.

27

In the army, they used to tell me: 'Gornostayev, you've got a killer's face.' I'd always thought of myself more as a pleasant, polite sort of man, but in the military people say the most incomprehensible things. It was only afterwards that I realized what the officers meant. Many people freeze under stress; they go into a panic, and it shows on their face. Not me. I feel the rush of adrenaline and fear, and a flurry of images run through my head, but at the same time my thoughts become brighter, clearer, faster and more focused – and an expressionless poker face takes over.

When Colonel Vikulov told me I was being enlisted into Special Forces and sent to Afghanistan, I listened impassively and stared at a spot on the wall just above his head. I didn't moan or complain; I didn't even blink. I said simply that it is our duty to protect the Fatherland wherever the Fatherland most needed our service. Vikulov approached me. He bit the edge of his mug and stared at me, his eyes a mere three centimetres from my face, and started to laugh. 'Damn it, Gornostayev, you don't think we'd really send you across the mountains to be slaughtered, do you? We're making you a ski instructor, and while you're abroad we'd like you to observe more than just the quality of the snow.'

Colonel Vikulov had saved me – but now I was on my own, surrounded by troops from the wrong army. I managed to keep my face deadpan and my thoughts clear. I couldn't let my imagination run wild; there was only a single thought in my mind. But that thought was beating at my skull like an anvil: you've been had, Kärppä, and not just once.

'Get packing,' said Ryshkov. 'Those boxes of phones are being moved to the truck. We've got other stuff for the Volkswagen.' He started lifting plastic-wrapped boxes onto the back of the Mitsubishi by himself.

I began lifting as well. Nokia boxes the size of bricks had been packed in their dozens into a single unit. Through the plastic wrapping I could see the boxes of telephones and Styrofoam packaging. I lifted the mobile phones onto the truck. I saw that Jaak Lillepuu had finished his conversation and was now sitting fully on the desk, swinging his legs beneath it and talking to his sister. Sirje was quiet and expectant, listening, chuckling at something Jaak had said. They were speaking Estonian. I couldn't hear them properly or understand what they were saying. I tried not to stare at them, though I'd rarely seen two dead people in such fine fettle.

'Explain this to me,' I said to Ryshkov under my breath, and continued lifting boxes into the truck. 'Who have you killed? And what about Aarne Larsson? Did he kill anyone? And who were those bodies?'

'That's a lot of questions,' he replied. 'Well, they were a brother and sister from Moldova. Getting hold of two people who looked like Jaak and Sirje took a bit of finding. And we had to dye the girl's hair. She was a hooker, and the guy was her retarded brother. We employed them here for a while, but their contract was pretty short.'

I listened. I attempted to work out the scenario, trying not to think that these Moldovans had had names, and a mother and father somewhere. I focused on taking in what Ryshkov was telling me.

'The police took samples and confirmed their identities,' he continued. 'I should say, they established that the deceased were brother and sister. And the Tallinn police came up with a suitable set of dental records.'

Ryshkov put down his box, straightened his back and looked me in the eyes, almost gently. He leaned his head to one side and spoke at greater length than he had for a month.

'Viktor, you're an intelligent man, you speak foreign languages, you're not the average dumb crook. Neither am I – and neither are these men. You'd be well advised to get along with them. We're going to be doing big business together. I vouched for you. You've been on this case for a lot longer than you know. And Aarne Larsson didn't come up with your name by chance. Sirje wanted to get rid of her crazy old man, so she left him. Jaak told his brother-in-law about you, said you were good at tracking people down. But then Aarne started to suspect things weren't quite kosher. He probably suspected his father-in-law, so he had to be neutralized.'

The warehouse door opened suddenly, interrupting Ryshkov's monologue. The two Estonian-looking men loading tracksuits into the Volkswagen stopped on the spot and almost stood to attention. Jaak Lillepuu jumped down from the table, and even Ryshkov stood like a lower-ranking officer in a parade turning to face the general.

I realized that the boss had arrived. Lillepuu the Elder stepped inside.

Paul Lillepuu paced around the warehouse as though he were inspecting the bed-making skills of some young recruits. He stopped and stood for a moment, his back straight and his hands behind his back, then moved a few metres briskly and spoke. I made out words in Russian and Estonian.

Lillepuu stopped next to us. He had to look up at me, but I got the impression this was more of a problem for me than it was for him.

'Well. Welcome to our little group. Ryshkov has told me good things about you. Remember, we trust you.' Lillepuu seemed to force his voice, making it lower and manlier, and didn't stand around to hear whether I had anything to say in reply. He turned away and told those present to get a move on.

I continued lifting boxes, stepped up onto the back of the truck and started rearranging things to make the boxes fit better.

'Are these phones fake?'

'No. We're just transporting them.'

Ryshkov leaned against the lifting platform, paused for thought and decided to explain what was going on.

'The phones are legit. But the boxes are ours. We put the goods in aluminium boxes, the boxes go into a mould and we pour Styrofoam round the outside. Then we attach the boxes with the mobile phones and wrap everything up in plastic. It doesn't smell, doesn't show and it won't break. Nice and tidy.'

'What goods?' I asked, though I knew perfectly well.

'A small consignment of heroin, street value of about three million marks. It depends how we get it distributed. It's been refined at one of our own labs.'

Ryshkov sounded proud, and nodded towards the back wall of the warehouse. All I could see was empty shelf space.

'It's over there,' he explained. I nodded and turned my back to him, lifted more boxes and continued organizing them in the back of the truck. If Colonel Vikulov could see my face now, I thought, he would send me to Chechnya in a flash. I was sure my expression now betrayed shock and fear. At the same time, I wondered why the compliments from Ryshkov and Lillepuu had felt so good.

28

We headed for the harbour. Ryshkov was sitting in the passenger seat of the Volkswagen van, and Lillepuu's minder, who had introduced himself as 'Kardo', was driving. They were to enter the ferry and disembark before me. The van was packed with Adidas tracksuits manufactured in Estonia and a few boxes of CDs. The goods were legal, but looked suspicious. If the customs officials were keen, they would stop a man like Ryshkov and investigate his dodgy-looking cargo. And I, with my honest Finnish face and passport, would drive my shiny new car through Customs a few cars later.

The other Estonian with us, Mart, came to the harbour in my car, but he was to get off the ship via the passenger ramp. I followed the Volkswagen through the unfamiliar streets, gripping the steering wheel, my hands turning tacky with sweat. *Think, Viktor, think,* I told myself.

Once at the harbour, we were forced to queue because there were a lot of trucks going onto the ferry first. 'Wonder if the ladies have been missing me,' I commented breezily to Mart. 'Any messages?' I thought I must have sounded fake, but fiddled with my phone, leaving the keypad unlocked. I put it back in my jacket pocket. Mart looked at me long and hard. I wondered whether he was keeping an eye on me or just thought I was an idiot.

I saw Ryshkov stepping out of his car and walking up to our door. I wound down the window. He leaned towards us.

'There's a pistol under the seat, just in case. Make sure it's within easy reach.'

I fumbled beneath the seat until my hand touched the cold steel and the grooved plastic plates at the back. I pulled the weapon into the leg space. It was an FN 9-millimetre, its steel body almost a shade of blue. I nodded and carefully replaced the pistol underneath the seat.

'Viktor. This shipment must be delivered in one piece,' said Ryshkov, his voice serious. He gripped my arm gently but firmly, and walked back to his Volkswagen. I nodded and wound the window back up.

I switched on the radio. Mart sat next to me, staring ahead. I put my left hand inside my pocket and began pressing the buttons on my phone. First MENU, which I pressed with my thumb, then MESSAGES, then SELECT to bring up my inbox, then two upward clicks and the screen should read: NEW MESSAGE.

I repeated the instructions to myself, humming them in time with the music so that Mart wouldn't notice what I was up to.

Again, I pressed SELECT and calculated that now all I had to do was write. I felt the keypad with my thumb and tried to leave enough time between each letter. I cursed to myself that any high-school kid would have been able to send this message six times over within the same timeframe.

Keep calm, I told myself.

SERIOUS STUFF. FERRY AT 1800. TELL KORHONEN: BIG FISH.

Then I thumbed down to MENU. The phone offered me the option to send, and I clicked OK. After that, the telephone asked which number to send the message to. I pressed the up-and-down arrows until I got to the beginning of the alphabet – Marja's number was saved as AAA–Sweetheart. Then OK again, and the telephone showed the number; then OK one final time, and the phone informed me that the message had been sent.

A moment later I pressed the DELETE button. I waited for the screen to give me the EXIT button, pressed it twice and imagined I must be back at the main menu. I took out my phone to look at it as if in passing and saw SEARCH, OPTIONS, NEW and DELETE at the bottom of the screen. My calculations must have gone awry at some point, but I didn't know where.

At that moment, a flash of suspicion and bitter jealousy seared through my mind like a painfully bright light, hurting my eyes and head. If Ryshkov and Lillepuu had been giving me the runaround all this time, was Marja really all she seemed to be?

Ryshkov had reserved a cabin for the duration of the crossing. We would all be staying in it throughout the journey, he told us in clipped tones. I decided not to joke about wanting to jump in the ball pool, but grinned to myself: put a smile on your face though your heart might be breaking, Mother had always said. And suddenly there was nothing to laugh about.

We sat on the lower berth of the shabby cabin. The carpet filled the room with a fusty smell. It had been trampled on and stained by the feet of thousands of travellers determined to have fun, but with little inclination to clean up after themselves. Ryshkov and Kardo smoked while Mart and I slumped on the bunk. My mobile phone beeped, and everyone froze.

I took the phone out of my pocket. 'Text message,' I said inanely.

'Show me.' Ryshkov snatched my phone and gave it to Mart. 'Tell me what it says, in Russian.'

Mart read it, chuckled and translated: 'It says: *Don't think I'm coming to pick you up.* And the sender is "AAA–Sweetheart".'

I shrugged my shoulders and tried to make myself blush. 'I sent Marja a message telling her I was in Tallinn. This morning I told her I was going to Mikkeli. I think she's in a bit of a huff.'

Ryshkov looked at me for a long while, took the phone from Mart's hand and gave it back to me. Then he lifted his Diadora bag to the floor and began taking out some food. He laid the small table with bread, cheese, sausage, preserved meats, fresh cucumber, pickled gherkins, cans of beer and soft drinks, four glasses and a bottle of vodka. He twisted the bottle top open, poured vodka into all four glasses and handed them round. Ryshkov looked each of us in the eye in turn and raised his glass: '*Na zdorovie!*'

We drank and ate.

29

The air in the car deck was blue with diesel fumes. Romanians, Bulgarians, Latvians, Lithuanians, one after another each of the truck drivers revved their engines to life. The ferry staff waved to each line of vehicles in turn. I saw Ryshkov turn the ignition in his Volkswagen Transporter; the rear lights flickered and lit up. The Mitsubishi's diesel engine ignited with a quick flick of the keys, and I followed Ryshkov. I was sitting in the car by myself now, and again I was calm. As soon as we drove along the ramp and out onto the docking area, I opened the window and took a deep, calm, satisfying breath.

The queue of vehicles moved along slowly. I kept my head upright, but allowed my eyes to roam from one side of my field of vision to the other, slowly scanning from left to right and back again. I couldn't see any police or customs officials – nobody whose presence I sorely needed.

We were approaching the passport-control booth and customs. The customs officer took Ryshkov's papers, stepped behind the desk, examined his passport but soon returned, saluted and handed the papers back to him. I showed my Finnish passport and the police officer nodded, satisfied. We continued crawling along; the trucks found it hard to turn in the cramped forecourt, and I saw that Customs had decided to open one of the trailers towed behind the old Scania.

The Volkswagen accelerated in front of me. I tried to put my foot down in the Mitsubishi, and cursed to myself: was bringing heroin into the country this easy? It was then that I saw the blue flashing lights. At that, the Volkwagen's brake lights lit up, bright red; the car swerved to one side, and Ryshkov dashed out of the car.

He crouched down and hopped towards my car. I could see he was holding his right hand inside his jacket. Behind the Volkswagen flashed the lights of two police cars, and officers in blue uniforms were running into position behind the concrete pillars of the customs building. I saw they were armed with what looked like submachine guns or assault rifles.

I reached for the weapon tucked at the back of my trousers. Ryshkov wrenched open the Mitsubishi's door and found himself staring right down the barrel of my pistol.

'Oh, Viktor... Viktor. What a childish thing you've done,' he sighed, but his voice gradually turned to nothing more than a hiss, betraying a mixture of anger, frustration and contempt.

'You're the one that's fucked here,' he said. 'The cargo is in your name. I'm getting out of here, nice and quiet.' He smiled at me. Again I caught a flash of his golden tooth. 'You could always shoot me,' he said. By now Ryshkov was laughing. 'But I didn't trust you enough to put any bullets in that gun.'

I raised my Chinese-copy weapon in two hands and aimed straight at Ryshkov's forehead.

'Good thing I never trust strange weapons,' I said, and watched his smile vanish.

The howl and wail of the sirens, the roar of the engines and the screeching of hydraulic brakes, the officers' clipped commands – everything melted into an unfathomable noise that seemed to wrap a hood around my head.

At the edge of my field of vision I was aware of the flash of lights, the dark blue uniforms dashing past, truck drivers running for cover behind the double tires of their trucks. But all this was happening around me, almost out of focus. I squinted and aimed right between Ryshkov's eyes, looking along the barrel of the pistol, keeping the slot and bead in a line that ended above his nose, at the spot where his brow furrowed and his eyebrows met one another.

I aimed like an Olympic shooter, though at half a metre a little less precision would have been enough. A 9-millimetre bullet would make a clean, crisp hole in the front of the face; then it would open out and use up the rest of its kinetic energy pummelling and tearing the tissue inside the skull before coming out the other side, taking the back of the head with it. And half of Gennady Ryshkov's brain too. And all his thoughts, consciousness and soul, if such a thing existed. Everything. Gone.

I thought of Gennady Petrovich Ryshkov, my employer and friend. I thought of how we had driven together. In the warm car that morning, it had felt almost pleasant. I had felt important, significant, as we took care of business together; we couldn't really call it 'work'. I'd done most of the talking; Gennady had simply chuckled, muttered in agreement. He rarely disagreed or raised his voice when giving orders. I thought of Yelena Ryshkova and their daughter, who only a while ago had been a scrawny girl at ballet school with plaits in her hair, and for whom Ryshkov was the only father she had. I thought of how I'd never been sent to Afghanistan or anywhere else where I might have been forced to kill people. I had never killed anyone, not even an unknown enemy fighter at a distance, neither in a legal war nor in obeying military orders that would have silenced any suspicion on my part.

Ryshkov focused, alternately, at the black eye of the pistol's barrel and at me. He was afraid, and squinted his eyes as though this would protect him from the shot. His mouth was slightly open, his tongue wetting his lips. Then, all at once, his eyes opened and the muscles of his face relaxed. Ryshkov's expression turned first to relief then to a look of victory, almost mockery.

'It doesn't matter whether it's loaded or not. You're not man enough to do it.' Fury flew from his mouth in droplets of spittle, striking me in the face. 'It's in your papers. Your intellectual make-up, emotional control and ability to tolerate pressure are good, it says, but you're unwilling to engage in extreme measures. A man with a killer's face? Pull the other one! You wouldn't do it.'

The barrel of my pistol had lowered, and was now pointing at Ryshkov's Adam's apple. I raised it again until it pointed directly between his eyes, which were so dismissive and enraged, and pressed the end of the pistol and gripped the trigger. I'd had enough.

The shot rang out like a fighter jet breaking the sound barrier on a calm summer day. The sound echoed between the concrete walls of the terminal and popped my ears open, so I could once again hear the noise of the commotion around me, the shouts, the squeal of rubber tires against the asphalt. I heard the screech of a bird flying away, a sound that didn't belong with the rest of the picture.

I stared at my falling pistol in dismay. I expected to see smoke rising from the barrel, and I was about the explain to the approaching officers that the trigger was too sensitive, that it had slipped in my hand, when I realized that someone else had fired the shot. With my thumb I flicked the safety catch back on, carefully replaced the gun beneath my belt and half-raised my hands out of the car.

Ryshkov was lying slumped on his side, his abdomen swollen like a giant seal. His mouth was open. I couldn't see where the bullet had struck him, but beneath the cheek touching the ground a pool of blood had formed, turning the tattered asphalt black.

A crush of policemen in dark-blue overalls swarmed around Ryshkov's body. A red Golf pulled up next to us, its brakes howling; a grey Mercedes approached from the front and came to stop just inches from the bonnet of the Volkswagen.

Out of the Golf stepped a man in his thirties, with a toned body and a fringe combed trendily to one side. He reminded me of a British footballer, though he was short for a policeman. He must have had to stretch himself to the limit to meet the height requirements at the academy. He looked at me disdainfully.

'Evening. Piirainen, from Homeland Security. Come along, Semyonov. You'll be going back to Russia before you know what's hit you.'

Piirainen from Homeland Security didn't bother shaking my hand. He looked as though he didn't expect me to respond. He took a few steps and clasped his hands together as though he'd rubbed them with soap.

'Well, Arkady, you've done us a real favour. But let *us* take care of things next time, okay? That's how things work in Finland these days.'

I realized he wasn't speaking to me, but to the man who had stepped out of the grey Mercedes. I also realized the car had diplomatic plates, and that the man was heavyset: his fur coat had been switched for a leather jacket, but the shoes were the same ones I'd seen him wearing when he'd spotted me outside Stockmann's.

'I know I'm wasting my breath with you, Arkady. You'll still do whatever the hell you like. Now fuck off back to Russia where you belong,' Piirainen continued.

Arkady simply nodded in reply, like a parent to a child asking for too much, as if to say, 'Yes, yes, next time, I'll think about it.' Arkady was carrying two red-covered passports. He looked at the inside pages, chose one of them and handed it to me. It was a diplomatic passport. I saw my own familiar photograph and the personal information I'd learned during my trip to Sortavala: Semyonov, Igor Sergeyevich, born in Vologda on 2 February 1963.

I leaned against the side of the car and watched as Arkady gave the other passport to a man walking past me. Only now did I see that it was Mart, Lillepuu's Estonian bullyboy who had been in my car. At least that's who I thought it was. Now I heard him speaking in Russian, and laughing with Arkady. Piirainen approached us and shook Mart's hand, and the circle of police around Ryshkov's body backed away, turned to Mart and seemed to stand to attention.

Mart was smoking a cigarette, sucking the smoke hungrily into his lungs, and his cheeks were ruddy. He was carrying a wooden briefcase, which I knew contained a moulded plastic interior with gaps for the long barrel of his pistol, a box of bullets, spare ammunition and cleaning equipment. What's more, now I knew it was Mart who had shot Ryshkov.

Arkady walked up to the Mercedes, opened the back door and gestured to me and Mart to get in. He held out his hand, palm facing upwards, and waited for me to give him my pistol. The inside of the car smelled new. It was quiet. Mart sat down next to me and rapped his fingers against the shiny surface of his briefcase.

As we drove away I caught another glimpse of a group of blue-uniformed police officers standing around Ryshkov's body, and of a sniffer dog as it hopped up onto the trailer behind the Mitsubishi, wagging its tail eagerly. Standing slightly further off, as though they were bystanders, I saw Korhonen and Parjanne leaning against their own Golf. Korhonen had his hands in his pockets. He was once again far too well dressed for the occasion, and looked more like a banker than a police officer in his long, dark-blue woollen coat and yellow scarf, with no hat on. His eyes followed us; he pursed his lips and shook his head faintly. His expression exuded silent disappointment; I didn't know whether he was disappointed in me, or because he'd been forced to watch events from the sidelines.

I couldn't think about it any longer. Arkady was driving us towards Ruoholahti, and I lay back against the headrest and closed my eyes.

30

We drove to Töölö in silence, along Mechelininkatu and past the cemetery, the army barracks and the white birches in Sibelius Park. We crossed Topeliuksenkatu, turned onto Nordenskjöldinkatu and stopped in front of the Russian Arts and Science Centre. Arkady got out of the car and a blond, Finnish-looking man in his thirties took his place in the driver's seat. His hair jutted out in all directions, unfazed by the barber's painstaking work and his own attempts to comb and wax it into submission. The skin on his neck was red, with spots ready to burst.

'Grigori Myshkin is our technology secretary in Finland,' Arkady said, introducing the man from the doorway. He continued, pre-empting my question. 'Myshkin will drive you to Zelenogorsk, where you can take it easy for a while.' Then, to Myshkin, he said, 'I'll come and pick up Viktor in a few days.'

Myshkin nodded in our direction, greeted us formally in Russian and turned the key in the ignition. The next time he opened his mouth was when we stopped at Vaalimaa.

'Checkpoint,' he said, stating the obvious.

The Finnish border guards gave our diplomatic passports a cursory glance. In their expressions I could see a mixture of respect and fear that would become mockery once we'd turned our backs. We continued without delay. Myshkin took out his mobile phone and made a call, drove and changed gears as he spoke, his head to one side pressing the phone between his cheek and his shoulder. On the Russian side of the checkpoint, the barriers rose up for us automatically and the border guards waved us through, gesturing for us to drive past the queue without stopping.

Myshkin turned outside the tax-free kiosk, left the engine running and quickly went inside to buy a few items. He handed the plastic bag to Mart and me in the back seat. We had dozed off as the car glided along the smooth highways on the Finnish side, but now that we'd crossed the border, we were juddering through the dark, trying to avoid potholes, on our way to Vyborg. We drank beer and ate mint chocolate. I said a few words to Mart in Russian, and I couldn't make out whether he was Estonian–Russian, Russian–Estonian or whether his nationality transcended traditional borders. I didn't care to ask.

Myshkin was a skilful driver, able to sense cars driving round sharp bends with their lights dimmed, and he scraped past the muddy verge to avoid heavy trucks that tried to commandeer both lanes of traffic. I was so familiar with this road that even in the dark I knew exactly where we were. 'Zelenogorsk,' I said aloud, and thought to myself in Finnish that we would soon be turning towards Terijoki. We didn't stop, but continued following the Baltic coast along the windy road to St Petersburg.

When we reached Komarovo, Myshkin slowed slightly, and in the darkness almost turned into the wrong yard. Then he said, in stiff Finnish, his Ls thick and Slavic: 'Here it is. Kellomäki.'

Myshkin drove directly through the narrow gate and into the garden outside a two-storey house. It was already early morning. The moon was almost full, and the air was dry and chilly. A couple of lanterns hanging outside the house lit the garden as best they could at 40 watts, and it seemed as though the low-lying darkness was absorbing the light into its black holes. The moon was bright and lit the sky.

I stretched my back, shook my shoulders and drew fresh air deep into my lungs. In the yard I could make out the silhouettes of a children's climbing frame, wooden trains half-buried in the mud, plastic cars, rubber balls with their colours faded and a set of bowls lying on its side.

An old woman in spectacles and a headscarf stepped outside; she had a jacket slung over her shoulders and a pair of sandals on her feet. The woman greeted us and welcomed us inside. She said she would show us to our rooms and give us something to eat. Mart and I went in. In the middle of the house was a large hallway with a mosaic-patterned parquet floor that must once have been a skilled craftsman's pride and joy. Now it was scuffed and cracked. From the hallway, a staircase covered in red carpet led upstairs and, behind a pair of glass doors, corridors led to both ends of the house.

Myshkin brought us our suitcases and said they contained everything we needed. The old woman showed us to our rooms, number eight for Mart and number eleven for me. The room was cool and damp, though the radiator was piping hot. On the bed was a thick, spongy, malformed mattress, dazzling white sheets that smelled of detergent and blankets with synthetic fibres that crackled with static. The room felt much taller than it was long or wide. Even the window seemed to stretch too far up the wall. There was a large television on the desk, and a gleaming, brown wardrobe seemed to cover most of the floor space.

The old woman approached the door, shook a set of keys and invited us to come and eat. She showed us into the cold dining room and laid the table with rye bread, watery butter, greasy slices of sausage, boiled eggs, pickled gherkins and tea. Myshkin joined us at the table and said he would be driving back in the morning. We ate, bade one another good night and went to sleep.

In bed I tried not to think about Marja, the money in my bank account or the emergency funds inside my left loudspeaker, my car and office and my Finnish passport, which Arkady had confiscated, saying he would get me back into Finland under my own identity.

And my mother: 'You Sortavala boys,' she used to say in Finnish whenever our misfortune was too great to grieve.

When I awoke in the morning, it felt as though I had slept without moving in the slightest; even my head had lain still, oblivious and devoid of dreams. I lay on my back, the two blankets pulled up to my chin. The sheets looked entirely uncrumpled.

The bag Myshkin had given me contained underwear, sport socks, T-shirts and an Umbro running jacket, a hat, a pair of ski gloves and a set of Nike trainers. The embassy's equipment service had looked up my size requirements in the archive. Perhaps nowadays they looked up information like this in an online database, bits winding their way through the ether from Moscow, full of important zeros and ones, information that, when it arrived at the embassy in Helsinki, meant: Nike trainers, size 43, wide front.

I ate breakfast by myself and went outside. Nobody asked where I was going or tried to keep an eye on me. I walked along a dry section of pine forest sloping gently down towards the shores of the Baltic Sea. Our hostess had told us the house had once been a summer retreat for the children of local factory workers. Nowadays it was used mainly by writers from St Petersburg and hosted meetings, social events, holidays and writing retreats. The local area was full of similar houses, roughcast or covered in wood panelling, small run-down *dachas* and larger villas and sanatoriums.

I jogged down to the shore. The light sand seemed to extend for kilometres in both directions. To the southeast I could make out the tall buildings on the island of Kronstadt, and the outskirts of St Petersburg in the distance. The tide had washed up a bottle of Polish shampoo, a length of thick hemp rope, labels from Styrofoam fish traps, plastic canisters (now faded and unidentifiable) and beautifully decorated boards and balk timbers.

I turned back towards the house, continued along the highway and walked along the gravelly edge of the railway tracks. The Elektrichka screeched past, in a whoosh of green. Through the smudged windows I could see that the local train was full of the expressionless faces of commuters. I imagined that in winter it would be packed with fisherman dressed for the cold weather, their bags bulging with *mormyshka* jigs and jars of larvae, packed lunches wrapped in grease paper and bottles of vodka. And in the evenings these same men would make their way back to the suburbs of St Petersburg, red-faced and blind drunk, with just enough small perches to make a pot of soup.

Among the old villas and dilapidated cottages were a few brand-new houses, with some still under construction. Their gardens were surrounded by brick walls several metres high; at the side of each wrought-iron gate was an electronic box with a keypad for entering a code, security cameras and a direct phone to invisible security guards. All that was visible of the houses themselves were strange, unidentifiable ledges and towers, steep roofs and dark windows. 'Gangster gothic', I remember someone once calling the style.

The people who owned these houses were probably in the same profession as Ryshkov. I tried to look like a harmless, uninterested passer-by. I didn't want a guy in a leather jacket to appear at one of those gates shouting, 'Hey, you look familiar! Who do you work for? And what the hell are you doing prowling around here?'

Back at the writers' retreat, lunch awaited me: tough, sinewy chicken and rice collected in stodgy lumps with fruit compote for desert. I ate alone. Myshkin and the Mercedes had disappeared from the driveway that morning. After lunch I knocked on Mart's door. I heard an obliging grunt, and opened it. Mart was half-lying on the bed, fully clothed, smoking a cigarette and drinking vodka. He was only on his first bottle, but it was already almost empty. He looked at me with heavy eyes, and I told him to carry on in peace and quiet. I closed the door behind me.

Arkady arrived the following morning, this time in an Audi with Russian plates. He knocked on my door, walked straight in and began talking at once.

'I've had instructions from Moscow. You're being moved aside. Someone's looking out for you – either that, or you've got friends in high places. It's a shame, Viktor, a real shame. For me, anyway. I'd already thought you could be very useful to me. Though this Ryshkov thing must have come as a bit of a surprise to you.'

He continued: 'At first we only had one man working for Lillepuu, and we had an agreement with the Finns to give them intel on a large shipment of stolen goods at some point in the future. But Ryshkov took you with him, you panicked and sent your girl a message, the girl contacted your friend the policeman, and Homeland Security found out about it, so Piirainen and I had to set the whole operation in motion.' It sounded like Arkady was trying to sing a nursery rhyme as he listed the course of events. Something about a man with a farm and lots of animals, and all the animals made different noises. I couldn't remember the name of the song, and it bugged me.

'Well, here are your documents, some cash and a train ticket,' said Arkady. 'Pack your things. You can keep the tracksuit.' He smiled at his own generosity. 'In half an hour a Toyota will arrive, and the driver will take you to Vyborg. You'll be home by evening. And remember: you still have to take care of the Mikkeli job.'

Arkady handed me a bundle of papers tied with a rubber band. It contained almost a thousand marks, a crumpled bunch of roubles and a return ticket from Helsinki to Vyborg and back. The outward journey had already been stamped. It didn't surprise me in the least when I looked at my own Finnish passport and saw that Viktor Kärppä had been stamped into the country two days ago.

'Thank you... all the same,' I managed to say. Arkady waved his hand, went to Mart's door – if that really was his name – and said he'd be sending him on a spa holiday to the Black Sea.

31

Korhonen was sitting backwards on the chair I reserved for clients. Or perhaps more accurately, the chair was backwards and Korhonen was facing forwards. He asked me for details over and over, making sure he had understood everything correctly. Every now and then he stood up, stretched and took a few steps towards the window. He was smoking in such a way that smoke rose in pretty patterns through the air in my office, lit only by the desk lamp. Then he walked back again, straddled the chair and leaned his chin against his fists, which he had propped against the back of the chair.

And so I explained, tried to tell him everything as openly and convincingly as I could, saying I had only been employed by Ryshkov and that I didn't know anything about Lillepuu and the drugs. More importantly, I tried to get Korhonen to believe that I only helped Arkady very infrequently, and that I wasn't a full-time agent.

'Let's assume I believe you this time. But if something about this logic starts to stink, then I'll be back, and we'll have a thorough investigation of these procedures and organizations. Then we'll see whose ass can withstand the retraining, eh,' Korhonen threatened me, dramatically rolling his Rs. 'Just you remember, Kärppä, that from now on you and I are even closer buddies than before. What I mean is: you're mine. Piirainen from Homeland Security would have an orgasm if he heard there was a double agent like you living down here in Hakaniemi. Getting you deported would be a piece of cake. So I recommend you grow a moustache and cut that mop of yours to fit in with the youngsters.'

Korhonen stood up and looked at me; his eyes were laughing, though his lips remained pursed, and he said in surprisingly well-enunciated English: 'This could be the start of a beautiful friendship.'

He nodded, and looked as though he was still savouring his words. At the door he turned to face me again. 'Listen, off the record, could you get hold of a pair of Russian army night binoculars? For a decent price, eh? I need to get my boy a confirmation present.'

'How many do you need?' I asked, and took the box from my filing cabinet.

Marja didn't have much stuff to move. The van I'd rented from Ruuskanen was only half-full. The bed, chairs and table at the new apartment on Sallinkatu fit Marja's eco-friendly austerity style as they were. A set of Lundia bookshelves, a microwave, a table and her desk were the largest items of furniture we had to move. Books, clothes, dishes and other bits and pieces filled half a dozen cardboard boxes. The entire move took less than half a day.

I had helped go through Ryshkov's estate delicately with a solicitor. The majority of his business affairs had been managed through different companies in which he had no official stake, or in which his stake had been weaselled away so effectively that none of the funds could be linked to his estate. To my surprise it turned out that the studio flat on Sallinkatu was registered in Karpov's name, and he didn't mind me finding a new tenant. Of course, Karpov quipped that there were many ways Marja could pay the rent – to which I replied that if he tried that, I'd be forced to nail him to the wall by his scrotum.

He moaned, saying I had old-fashioned ideas about morality, but as a wise man he would learn to live with them. What's more, he had adapted to his new business situation in only half a day. Now he was eagerly planning to open a radio station in Karelia, and dreamed of newspapers and a television station – a whole media empire.

I left Marja folding her pillowcases and told her I was going to the office. That evening I wanted to get to sleep early and leave for Mikkeli first thing in the morning.

'I still have a bit of business to take care of up there.'

'Then I'd better give you this in advance,' said Marja, and took a small package from her bag. 'Your birthday is not till tomorrow, but Happy Birthday all the same.'

Marja hugged me and gave me a gentle kiss. I opened the wrapping paper. It was Andrei Makine's novel *Dreams of my Russian Summers*.

'It's about a man who grows up far away in the Russian countryside, then moves to France, the clash of cultures and... Well, read it for yourself. I think you'll like it.'

I tried to look Marja in the eyes, at once both serious and warm, and told her how much I appreciated it.

I was sitting in my office and had just selected Mother's telephone number on my mobile phone when Karpov's assistant knocked on the door. He was carrying a cardboard box, and politely shook my hand. He told me at great length that he'd driven all the way from Sortavala, and that in the morning he was going to the harbour to pick up a brand new Chevrolet SUV for his boss.

'Your mother gave me this box and told me to let you know she's doing well. I'm to wish you good health and much success on your birthday,' the man said verbatim, like a little boy. Only a little parting bow was missing.

I thanked him, and he left. Carefully, I opened the box, which was wrapped in string and brown paper. The Karelian pies were piled up inside and wrapped in grease paper, still giving off the warmth of my mother's bread oven.

I clicked on Mother's number once again.